OUT IN THE COLD

A BLUE COLLAR HEARTS PREQUEL

KIKI CLARK

Cover Designer: Cate Ashwood www.cateashwooddesigns.com/

www.kikiclark.com

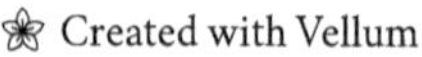

Out In The Cold

Being rescued by a hot lumberjack after catching his fiancé cheating was the only good thing to happen to Beau for quite some time.

Getting stuck in the man's cabin for the weekend? There were definitely worse ways to pass a few days.

Falling for him when the guy made it clear he didn't do relationships? Well, Beau just wouldn't do that… probably.

Out in the Cold is a 25k word novella with a 39-year-old furniture maker who is done with disappointing relationships, a 25-year-old accountant with terrible taste in fiancés but great taste in sexy underwear, a remote cabin in the woods during a snowstorm, and a rescue dog with more sense than his owner.

This one is for Marina.
Coop and Beau would not exist without you.

THE BLUE COLLAR HEARTS SERIES

Out In the Cold
(Beau & Coop)

Laying Pipe
(John & Lukas)

CHAPTER ONE

Standing at the threshold of his fiancé Danny's home office, Beau Singer suddenly understood why Danny always berated him for not knocking before entering. To be fair to himself, Beau usually *did* knock. It was just that sometimes he'd get so caught up in what he was doing or thinking or saying that he just acted without thinking.

Plus, Danny was his *fiancé*. Why did he need to knock on his office door before entering?

They'd be married soon, so they shouldn't have secrets from each other, right?

Wrong.

As Beau stared at his half-naked fiancé buried balls-deep in his assistant, the flyer for the new restaurant down the street fluttered to the ground from his lax fingers. He couldn't look away. Neither one had noticed him yet, too caught up in the throes of their sexual exploits to look up and see frumpy ol' Beau standing there staring.

Danny had never made love to him like that.

A hard ball of shame and anger and jealousy swirled in

the pit of his stomach. What the fuck did Danny think he was doing?

They were planning to get married in May! Why the hell was he fucking his assistant over the desk Beau's dad had bought him as an engagement gift?

Danny's assistant, Alexander, moaned what Beau felt was excessively loud and begged Danny to fuck him harder. That was it. He knew *for a fact* sex with Danny was not that good. A fact he'd been trying to ignore ever since Danny had proposed and Beau had accepted two months ago.

He'd told himself over and over again that it was okay if you never saw stars. He convinced himself that whole body shivers and being so satisfied and depleted that you passed out after you orgasmed was the stuff of movies and books.

He'd told himself that Danny was the best he could expect to do.

Well, that was bullshit. Being a little overweight and a tad boring did not mean he deserved *this.*

"Beau!" Danny screamed and stumbled backward. He'd apparently noticed him standing there while Beau had been busy realizing he deserved better than Danny's dumb ass. Beau stared dispassionately at Danny's slowly shriveling cock and then looked back at his assistant.

The skinny little twink was smirking at him upside down, not even bothering to let go of his erection.

"I'm going to stay somewhere else for the weekend," Beau said, voice weirdly calm. He figured this must be what people meant when they said they were having out-of-body experiences. His body and mind were numb and kind of… wavy along the edges? Like everything was and wasn't real at the same time. "Get all of your things out of my place by the time I get back Monday after work."

Eyes wide with shock—and probably a little fear—Danny scrambled to pull up his pants as he came around the desk, face transforming into one Beau was achingly familiar with: placation. "Sweetheart, don't do anything rash. I made a mistake and—"

He didn't bother to wait and hear any more. Turning on his heel, he strode across the large apartment to their bedroom, immediately going to the closet to pull down a small suitcase. His brain was tripping over itself, trying to process what he'd just seen, the implications for his life, and to not forget anything important while he threw some clothes, toiletries, and electronics together.

"Babe, this is silly. Let's be grown-ups and talk about this." Danny's patronizing voice sounded far away, Beau's heartbeat thundering in his ears so loudly it nearly drowned out the words.

Slowing, he squeezed the sweatshirt in his hands into a wrinkled mess as fury ripped through him. How many times had Danny said something like that to him? Made him feel immature or like he was overreacting because he was younger than Danny and his asshole friends?

He should have listened when his dad warned him about Danny the day he'd asked Beau out for their first date. But he'd been so swept off his feet by his charming smile and blatant flirting that Beau hadn't wanted to hear anything negative about the man. His dad had even come to grudgingly accept their relationship, gifting Danny with the desk he'd just been desecrating with Alexander's bare ass when Danny and he had moved in together after getting engaged.

"Are you even listening to me?" The stinging grip on his arm jolted Beau out of his thoughts, and he whipped around, shoving at Danny so hard he let go and fell to the ground, staring at Beau like he'd never seen him before.

"Don't touch me." Beau threw the sweatshirt into the suitcase and zipped it shut, figuring he'd buy anything he'd forgotten if he couldn't go without for a few days. "Get your shit out of here. I don't want to see you again."

Danny's artificially tanned skin flushed with anger as he stormed to his feet. "You're seriously going to break off our engagement because of one misstep?"

Dropping his suitcase by the door, Beau whirled around and stomped up to Danny. "Look me in the eye and tell me that this was the first time, that you were so drunk you had no idea what you were doing, that you tripped and fell into his ass. If you can tell me any of those things and mean it, I'll forgive you right now."

Danny studied his face closely, and Beau watched as he realized he couldn't just smooth things over this time. That he'd have to either come clean or lie to Beau's face. Shaking his head in disgust, Beau raked his eyes over Danny's rumpled form.

"You can't though, can you? If I hadn't come home early and caught you, you'd have kept sleeping with him and married me." He started to turn away, feeling gross just thinking about sharing a bed with Danny, when a thought occurred to him, and he looked back. "How long have you been sleeping with him?"

"Beau—"

"How. Long."

"Three months," a smug voice said behind him.

So since before Danny had hired Alexander and just after proposing to Beau.

He shut his eyes and wondered how he could have forgotten about the homewrecking assistant still in the apartment. Nodding like knowing how long they'd been sneaking around behind his back made any kind of sense and didn't make Beau want to cry for the first time since catching them, he opened his eyes and pegged Danny with the hardest look he could come up with.

Though that wasn't saying much considering he was generally seen as a marshmallow and pushover.

Not anymore.

"You're also going to want to look for another job," he said, voice harder than he was feeling. His bones felt brittle, like the slightest touch would crumble him into a million pieces, but he needed to get away from there before he could have a breakdown.

Danny snorted. "I'm the best project manager in the company. Your dad won't fire me."

They both knew that wasn't true, and the fear in Danny's eyes confirmed it. Smiling, Beau didn't bother arguing. He strode across the room as confidently as he could, grabbed his suitcase, and pushed past a gaping Alexander in the doorway.

"Does that mean I'm losing my job too? What the fuck, Danny?" Alexander screeched behind him just as Beau opened the door.

Rolling his eyes, he decided they might just deserve each other.

As he slammed the door shut, he began to wonder where the hell he was going to go. How could he look any of his friends in the face and tell them he'd caught Danny fucking someone else?

Biting his lip to hold back his tears, he headed down the hallway, realizing there was only one place he could go.

Home.

"What do you mean you aren't at home?"

His voice was a little higher pitched than he'd care to admit, but this was the absolute worst day for his dad not to be available for him to complain to while they ate ice cream at the island in his dad's pretentiously large kitchen.

That was all he wanted.

But apparently, the universe wasn't done screwing him over.

"Sorry, kiddo," his dad said, sounding genuinely remorseful and a little hesitant. "Did you and Danny get in a fight or something?"

Sighing, he turned on his blinker to change lanes so he could take the next right. He was on Woodward Avenue, just outside of Detroit, heading to his dad's place in Bloomfield Hills, but if his dad wasn't actually there, then his plans just changed. None of the people he called friends were the kind of people he'd want to show up on their doorstep unexpectedly, and most were more coworker than true friends.

Which was sad in and of itself.

Fuck, how did his life get to this place?

"Beau?"

Oh right, his dad was still on the line waiting for some sort of explanation as to why he'd called him near tears to make sure he'd be there when Beau arrived, ice cream in hand.

"I wouldn't call it a fight, no," he murmured, carefully maneuvering around Friday evening traffic in the Lexus his dad had gifted him when he'd graduated from college. "I would say we aren't together anymore."

He was nearly to the on-ramp for I-75 before his dad said anything. "I'm not sure how to respond here. Should I try and talk you out of calling things off or console you over it being over?"

God, he loved his dad. When it came to business, Garrett Singer was an absolute shark, but with his kid? Supportive teddy bear was the only way Beau could ever think to describe it.

When Beau came out, when he decided to pursue accounting instead of business because he didn't want to take over his dad's company one day, when his roommate in college spread a vile rumor about him, so he had to fight with the university to let him transfer dorms, and even when he started dating Danny, his dad had always been there and always backed him up. No matter what.

"I found him screwing that new assistant of his, so console, please. Also, I'm going to need you to fire both of them on Monday, okay?" His voice was a little wobbly by the end, his composure finally cracking now that he was talking about what had happened.

"What! That piece of shit!" his dad exploded, curses flying as he threatened everything from ruining Danny's career to beating the shit out of him.

By the time he wound down, Beau actually felt a little better. When the shock had started to wear off, he'd kept hearing Alexander's moans on repeat in his head, and it had been starting to get to him. His dad's anger on his behalf soothed a little of the pain he felt deep in his chest.

Taking an audible breath, his dad finally said, "I'm so sorry, Beau. And I'm really fucking sorry I'm not at the house. You can still go stay there. I'll head out first thing in the morning and be there by brunch."

Beau smiled and wiped at the stupid wetness on his cheeks. "It's fine. I'll just go up to the cabin. I might even stay next week too and just work remotely. I bet my boss will be okay with that."

His dad wasn't *technically* his boss since he was the owner and CEO of the company. Beau was just one of several accountants who worked for Singer Development, but the CFO, who he actually answered to, was also his godmother, so he wasn't too worried.

"What? No. Not with this snowstorm moving across Lake

Michigan. It's supposed to hit the shoreline in an hour and dump like a foot or more of snow. Just go to the house."

His dad was getting his bossy, I'm-in-charge-so-do-as-I-say voice, and Beau was *not* here for it. "I'll be fine. I've lived in Michigan my whole life—I think I can handle a little snow."

"Beau—"

"Dad, no. I'm going. I want to be… away from all this crap." Even at twenty-five, he hardly ever told his dad *no* when he'd dug in about something, but Beau was so exhausted he couldn't have a calm conversation about it and try and coax him into seeing reason.

He was pretty sure his dad muttered something under his breath about obstinate children, but Beau chose to ignore it.

"Fine. But if it starts getting bad, just get a hotel room somewhere and wait it out, okay?"

Smiling, he changed lanes to go around a slow semi. "Sure thing."

He wouldn't need to do that though. Like he'd said, he was confident in his ability to drive through a little bit of snow, and he'd be at his dad's cabin long before any real accumulation happened.

His dad was such a worrier, but Beau knew what he was doing. He'd spend a week mourning the loss of a relationship he never should have agreed to in the first place, then he'd go home, and that would be that.

He'd be able to get back to his easy, solitary life like the last year hadn't even happened.

And that was… great.

Right?

CHAPTER TWO

There was a car creeping down Coop Frances's driveway.

As he peered around his curtain, he could just barely make out the headlights with how heavy the snow was coming down.

Who the fuck would be dumb enough to be out driving in this weather, and why the hell would they be visiting him?

Trucker whined next to him, tail thumping against his leg because the traitorous dog loved visitors.

"They must be lost," he muttered. Trucker barked once and danced in place, even more excited, it seemed. "Settle down. They won't be staying to give you any attention, glutton."

Telling Trucker to stay, he pulled on his red plaid coat, black knit hat, and heavy winter boots and stepped out onto the tiny porch on the front of his cabin. He only used the place when he came up north to hunt or fish or occasionally get away from his nosey sister trying to pressure him into going on a date with her dentist… again.

Coop had been there and done that, and while the sex had been fine, he supposed, it hadn't been worth a repeat.

Not that Coop did repeats.

Repeats meant getting emotionally attached, and Coop didn't do that anymore. He was too set in his ways to try and turn his life upside down to accommodate another person. Being forty next year meant he was allowed to be, as his sister called it, a "grumpy old man."

He wasn't going to even step off the porch before sending the trespasser on their way, but when the overhead light came on as the engine turned off and he spotted pale, round cheeks and messy blond waves, he found himself edging closer to the top of the stairs.

The driver's-side door popped open, and the car was close enough that he heard the young man muttering to himself, though he couldn't quite make out the words. The guy took two steps away from his car—two steps too many; why wasn't Coop telling him to get lost already?—and somehow managed to trip and fall in the snow, landing on his hands and knees.

"Fuck," Coop spit out, hurrying down the stairs and rushing over to the young man. It didn't seem like he had moved an inch since hitting the ground, and worry began to fill him. Crouching next to the guy, Coop hesitantly set a gloved hand on his shoulder. "You okay?"

Wet laughter was the only response he got for a long moment, and then he raised his head to peer up at Coop, and the cold air froze in Coop's lungs. *Fucking hell.* The guy was gorgeous. Even red-rimmed and sad, the man's chocolate-brown eyes were piercing. His pale white skin was a little rosy from the subzero temperatures but looked so smooth Coop had to stop himself from reaching out and running a finger across his cheekbone.

"Worst. Day. Ever," the guy croaked out, then reached up

and gripped Coop's arm—why was he still touching his shoulder?—and used his hold to pull himself upright. He was a little thing, Coop could tell, but he straightened his shoulders like that would make a difference under his puffy coat and said, "Do you think I could stay here until the storm lets up? Then I'll get out of your hair."

"Um." What could he even say to that? Who just asked something like that of a stranger? What if he were an ax murderer? This sweet, trusting man could be dead long before the snow stopped falling.

The longer he hesitated, the less sure the man looked until finally his shoulders crumpled and his head dropped to his chest. "You're right. I'm sorry. I can just wait in my car. I have like half a tank of gas left, so I should be fine. Even if I run out, I've got a bunch of extra clothes I could put on, so I'm sure it's fine. I'm fine."

The guy was the opposite of fine.

And he'd freeze to death if left on his own out in the cold.

Shaking his head, Coop pushed himself to his feet and dragged the guy up with him. He eyed his soaked pant legs and grunted. "Get your things."

Face brightening, the guy scrambled back over to his car, opened the back door, and pulled out a suitcase. "Thank you so much. I promise you won't even know I'm here," he rambled as he slammed the door shut and hurried after Coop, who was already climbing the porch steps. "I can just sit by the door and read on my phone. I'll be the least obtrusive guest you've ever had. I'm sure the snow will stop soon, and then I can just—puppy!"

Trucker was beside himself as they stepped inside the cabin, the guy immediately dropping to his knees again and wrapping his arms around Trucker's wiggling body. Sighing, Coop stepped around them and divested himself of his outerwear, stepping back into his slippers and heading into the tiny kitchen.

"You need to change out of your wet clothes," he said, trying not to grumble at the guy but failing. As cute as he was, the man was invading Coop's private space because he wasn't smart enough not to be out driving in a blizzard.

He pulled the milk out of the fridge and a saucepan from a cupboard. When the guy laughed behind him, he sighed and turned around to tell him to go and change again.

Somehow the guy had ended up on his back, still in his puffy coat, with Trucker lying on top of him, licking at his face. Considering Trucker was eighty-five pounds, Coop knew for a fact it wasn't comfortable to have him crawling around on top of you, but the guy looked like he was in heaven, whispering to him what a good boy he was and how sweet and gorgeous.

Coop stared at them for a long moment, trying to figure out the feeling spinning in his gut. Was he… jealous of his own dog?

"What's your name?" he bit out, sounding angry for some reason even though he wasn't.

The guy flinched and sat up, gently pushing Trucker down so he was draped over his legs like the German shepherd mix was a damn lap dog. "Um, Beau?"

Raising a brow, Coop crossed his arms. "You sure about that?"

With an adorable scowl, the guy pushed his errant hair away from his face and lifted his chin. "Yes. Beau Singer."

Biting back a smile, Coop nodded. "Cooper Frances." He dipped his head toward his ridiculous dog. "That's Trucker."

Beau's frown disappeared as quickly as it had arrived. Leaning over Trucker, he wrapped his arms around him again and peppered kisses on his head. "Aww, what a cute name for such a sweet boy."

He watched Beau lavish affection on Trucker for another minute or so and then rolled his eyes. "Beau. Go change your clothes."

With a ridiculously heavy sigh, Beau gave Trucker's head one more kiss, and then he tried to gently coax the dog off his lap. Which, of course, Trucker was having none of now that he'd found someone who'd worship him like he thought he deserved.

Coop snapped his fingers, and Trucker jumped up, coming right over to his side and sitting. Beau rose slower, eyeing Trucker like he'd never seen a dog before. Once he was on his feet, he finally unzipped his coat and toed off his boots.

Satisfied, Coop went back to what he was doing. "You allergic to dairy?"

There was a thump behind him, but no verbal response.

Sighing again, he turned around again and nearly swallowed his tongue at the sight of Beau bent over at the waist, digging through his suitcase. While his khakis were a little baggy when he was standing, the position gave Coop a clear view of what a nice round ass he had with hips sturdy enough to take a real—

He stopped that train of thought before it could go further, reaching down to rearrange his semi-hard dick.

He could hear faint muttering that got louder as Beau started pulling out items and stacking them on the floor next to the case.

"Son of a biscuit," Beau finally said, throwing down what looked like… a dress shirt?

"Problem?"

Turning slowly, Beau bit his lip and stared at the ground between them. "Um, no?"

Rubbing at the headache forming in his temples, he took a deep breath and let it out slowly. "Listen. We don't know each other, but lying is a thing for me, okay? Just tell me what the problem is so I can fix it."

Beau chewed on his lower lip for a couple seconds, eyes getting a little glassy. "I… I didn't pay attention to what I was packing, and I didn't grab any pants."

"You didn't… grab any pants." Coop repeated the words, but they still didn't make sense to him.

Beau shook his head forcefully, blond waves flying around his head with the hard motion. Coop waited to see if he'd say anything more, like maybe explain how he could have left his house with a suitcase full of shirts, but the color in his cheeks said he was too embarrassed.

Shrugging, Coop strode toward the back of the cabin where the door to the bedroom was. The whole place was only two rooms, really. The front of the cabin made up the kitchen and living room, and the back was the bedroom and bathroom. It wasn't a lot, but it was plenty for just him and Trucker.

In his bedroom, he went over to the dresser and pulled open the drawer he kept his sweats and long johns in. He didn't understand how a person could pack a suitcase and not include any pants, but he was getting the feeling Beau maybe didn't work like other people.

And he *did not* find that charming.

Honestly.

Turning back toward the door, he stumbled to a stop when he realized Beau was standing just inside his bedroom, looking more unsure of himself than he had even when kneeling in the snow outside asking to take shelter in Coop's cabin. Trucker was leaning against his leg, looking up at Beau adoringly, but Coop found he didn't mind as much now that he knew what a mess Beau was.

"Here you go," he said, voice soft but still gruff. He held out the sweats. They were the only ones he had with him with an actual drawstring. Hopefully, Beau would be able to tighten them enough to stay up since he was a lot shorter than Coop's tall frame.

"Thank you," Beau whispered, accepting the pants but not moving out of the way, so Coop leaned against the dresser and shoved his hands in his pockets, waiting to see what else he had to say. Finally, Beau blurted out, "I'm not usually like this."

"Okay…"

"I mean… I am, but not to this extent. Or well…" Groaning, Beau rubbed at his eyes, taking in a shuddery breath. With his eyes still covered, he whispered, "I found my fiancé screwing his assistant a few hours ago. So things are kind of terrible right now."

Some of Coop's annoyance began to melt away. He knew from experience how easy it was to make dumb decisions when you were hurting from a betrayal like that. "That must have been painful."

Beau did a weird nodding shrug thing that Coop wasn't sure how to interpret. "I just… I wanted you to know that I'm not usually so dumb, okay? I should have listened to my dad about the snowstorm, but I just wanted to get as far away from Danny and his stupidly perfect assistant as I could. And with Danny following me through our apartment as I was trying to pack, I didn't pay attention to what I was grabbing."

This Danny sounded like a real piece of work.

"You found them having sex in your apartment, or he followed you to your apartment and then inside?"

Beau's hands dropped to his sides, and he gave Coop a look that said he really didn't think that question was relevant, but he answered it anyway. "In our apartment. Danny has—*had* an office in the second bedroom, and he worked out of it sometimes." He shrugged loosely, his arms flopping around a little, and continued as his eyes traveled around

Coop's bedroom curiously. "His assistant didn't usually come over, but it wasn't completely unheard of, so I didn't even think twice about his car in our guest parking spot. But there they were, right on top of Danny's desk. His skinny little assistant moaning like Danny actually..."

He trailed off as he bit his lip, meeting Coop's eyes for only a second, then dropping his gaze to Trucker, cheeks flushing adorably. There was something in his voice, though, that had Coop taking half a step closer.

Fuck. He had to be reading into it, but it almost sounded like cute little Beau was more upset at being cheated on than his engagement ending.

And also like Danny might have been lousy in the sack.

As tempting as it was to offer Beau a shoulder to cry on—or his dick to bounce on in revenge—that vulnerable look in those chocolatey eyes spelled trouble. Coop would bet his cabin and all the land it sat on that Beau wasn't a one-night-stand kind of guy.

But one night was all Coop had to offer anyone anymore.

CHAPTER THREE

Beau was such an idiot.

He'd meant to calmly explain to Cooper that he'd had a terrible day and wasn't always so absentminded or careless, and then he'd blurted out the embarrassing bits and outed himself in the process. Cooper hadn't seemed to care, even offering a brief shoulder squeeze and a gruff, "He sounds like a piece of shit," before heading back to the front of the cabin after confirming Beau wasn't allergic to milk for some reason.

Closing the door to the rest of the cabin, Beau stood in a strange man's bedroom and wondered what the hell he was doing.

When the snow had gotten so bad he could barely see on the highway, he'd taken the first exit he could and looked for a place to stay, but there'd been nothing. Maybe he'd turned the wrong way at some point, but he'd only seen a gas station, two fast-food places, and a big-box store whose parking lot was mostly empty.

But no motels.

He'd traveled farther down the road and away from the

highway, thinking he'd maybe come across an actual town at some point, but the lights became fewer and farther between, and it got so he couldn't see more than a few feet in front of his front bumper. Real fear had clenched his gut.

Then he'd spotted a driveaway, and even though any tire tracks had been filled, he could tell by the mounds on the sides that it had been recently plowed.

So he'd turned down it, praying he'd find help at the end and not just a run-down cabin without heat or a terrifying redneck with a shotgun.

Instead, he'd found Cooper Frances.

The only lucky thing to happen all day. While he was a little… gruff, he'd opened his home to Beau and had the sweetest dog in the world. Trucker had actually sealed the deal for Beau on trusting Cooper not to murder him while he slept or anything. An evil person couldn't have such a nice dog, right?

Shivering, he realized he was really starting to get chilled. He quickly undid his belt and pants and let his khakis drop to his ankles, stepping out of them. Bending to pick them up, he frowned as he looked around for a place to lay them out to dry. He ended up in the bathroom, draping them over the edge of the tub and hoping Cooper wouldn't mind.

He scowled at the damp edges of his long sleeves. After everything else, falling in the snow had really been the cherry on top of an absolutely awful day. Sighing, he unbuttoned his sleeves and then down his front, leaving his work shirt with his pants and returning to the bedroom in nothing but his tiny, light blue panties.

Danny had once told him his choice of undergarments was the only interesting thing about him. He'd said it like he was joking, and Beau had laughed it off, but now he knew it was probably the truth. Or, at least, that was how Danny had seen him.

"Well, screw him," Beau muttered fiercely, grabbing the sweats from where he'd placed them next to his sweatshirt on the end of the bed.

He was bent over, stepping into the sweats, when the door opened behind him. He tried to turn around and pull the material up his legs and step behind the corner of the bed all at the same time.

All he managed to do was fall on his ass.

An awkward throat cleared above him, but he refused to open his eyes. If he didn't look, then it wasn't true; he wasn't lying on the floor at Cooper's feet in nothing but his underwear, borrowed sweatpants tangled around his feet.

"You okay?"

Sighing, he opened one eye into a slit and peered at Cooper upside down, absently petting Trucker when he lay next to Beau and nudged at his arm. "No. My ego can't take much more."

It was hard to tell from the angle and because of Cooper's short beard, but it looked like he was smiling at Beau a little. "Somehow, I think it can take it. Where are your keys?"

"What?" He sat up and straightened the sweats, pulling them up to his knees, then standing and pulling them up the rest of the way. When he realized Cooper hadn't explained himself, he turned back to him and saw he was frowning at the sweats. Beau glanced down, tugging at where the material clung to his hips and ass. They were too long but otherwise fit well enough to do. He could feel his face turning red as he tried not to think about what Cooper must be thinking about his underwear. "What's wrong?"

"Nothing," Cooper rasped, turning away and rubbing at the back of his neck. "Your keys?"

"Um." He uselessly felt the pockets of the sweats as he tried to remember if he'd brought them inside. "Maybe my pants. Hang on."

They were still in the pocket of his khakis. He jingled them at Cooper as he returned to the bedroom, smiling triumphantly.

"Got 'em!"

Cooper accepted them with raised brows. "Congratulations?"

"What do you need them for?" A dark thought occurred to him. "You're not going to dismantle my car or something so I can never leave, right?"

Oh god. One tepid smile, and he'd just handed over his keys without a second thought. He *was* an idiot!

"I come here to get away from people," Cooper explained slowly, like Beau should just know that and him suggesting Cooper might want to keep him there for nefarious purposes was insane.

Maybe he was going insane. Maybe the entire awful day was just some sort of hallucination. That would explain why he found Cooper's grumpiness adorable instead of off-putting or even terrifying, right? The whole situation should be scaring the crap out of him, and instead, he couldn't help but wonder if the clingy sweats made his ass look huge.

"Um. Right. Okay. So why...?"

"You left your headlights on," Cooper said over his shoulder as he strolled back out of the room.

Slapping a hand to his face, Beau tried to decide if it would be better for him to just hide out in the bathroom the rest of the night rather than face Cooper and risk embarrassing himself continuously.

He pulled on his sweatshirt—one he'd had since he was in college and wouldn't get rid of until it fell apart because it was so comfortable—then tiptoed out of the bedroom, Trucker plastered to his side.

Just as he was considering whether it would be presumptuous to sit on the couch or not, Cooper opened the front door, stomping his feet clean of snow as he entered. There were flecks of snow on his hat and plaid coat, letting Beau know it was still coming down out there.

"Thank you," he murmured, accepting his keys once Cooper had stripped out of his outerwear. "I would have panicked if I couldn't start my car in the morning."

Cooper didn't say anything for a while, heading into the kitchen and pouring something from a saucepan into a mug. There was a faint aroma of chocolate in the air, and it made Beau's stomach growl. He hadn't bothered stopping for dinner, not really hungry when he'd first left Detroit and then not wanting to stop because of the snow.

He was definitely regretting all of his life choices at the moment.

When Cooper turned around and found Beau still hovering in the middle of the living room, tugging at the long sleeves of his sweatshirt, he frowned. "You can sit down."

He nodded numbly and collapsed into the corner of the large, comfy sofa, suddenly feeling overwhelmed and exhausted. What was he doing? He should have just gone to his dad's house or kicked Danny out of his apartment instead of fleeing. What if Danny was still there when he got back? What if Cooper was only pretending to be nice but tortured and killed him later that night after gaining Beau's trust? What if he'd only borrowed the keys to sabotage something in the engine? What if—

A warm, soft body pressed against him, and a cold nose nudged at his jaw, drawing him out of his panicky spiral and back into the living room. Cooper was crouched in front of him, dark blue eyes filled with what looked like concern, deep ridges between his thick brows.

"Are you okay?" Cooper asked, his voice a little softer

than normal but still kind of husky. "You were nearly hyperventilating."

He pulled Trucker farther onto his lap and wrapped his arms around the fluffy dog, burying his embarrassed face into his fur. "I'm fine," he said, voice muffled, then remembered Cooper's *thing* about lying. "I mean, I'm not fine. But I'm feeling better. I was just… Have you ever wondered how you got to a certain place in your life? Like, what decision did you make as a kid that led you down the path that ended in this horribly painful moment?"

Eyes widening for a moment, Cooper almost looked like he was trying not to laugh as he extended the steaming mug he was holding to Beau and scratched at his whiskered cheek. "You don't look old enough to have that many regrets, Beau."

"Twenty-five-year-olds can have regrets," he exclaimed, gingerly accepting the hot chocolate, even though he couldn't see well around Trucker's big body. "Though… most of mine tend to revolve around the men I date."

Humming, Cooper pushed to his feet and gestured at the mug. "Drink your cocoa and stop freaking out. The snow isn't stopping anytime soon, so we're stuck together for a couple of days probably."

A couple of days? Absently, he did as ordered, taking a careful sip of the hot liquid and then moaning. "Oh my god, this is amazing. Way better than when I make it with water."

"Water?" Cooper looked honestly offended at the idea.

Beau bit his lip. "Wow. That was some hard-core judgment. And people call me pretentious…"

"Who calls you that?"

Waving a hand, he took a bigger drink, letting his eyes fall closed as the sweet warmth filled him, heating him from the inside out. He sighed happily as he relaxed for the first time in hours. No way was he going to bring up Danny and his crappy friends or the fake friends he'd had in high school. He'd thought he'd learned by now how to spot people who looked at him and only saw his dad's money, but Danny proved he was still easily fooled.

He thought Cooper had wandered away again, so he jumped a little when he spoke from the same spot in front of Beau, and his eyes popped open.

"Did you eat?" Cooper was frowning again, studying Beau and obviously finding him lacking.

He wasn't the first person.

"No, but you don't have to make me something. If it's okay with you, I'm sure I can find something when I'm done." He tried to sound firm and in control, like he didn't regularly forget to eat or trip over piles of dirty clothes that would accumulate if Danny wasn't around to pester him into doing laundry.

And don't even ask how many dishes he'd thrown away because they'd sat so long and gotten so gross he'd decided it was easier to buy new than try and clean them.

He was a work in progress, okay?

Cooper grunted like he didn't believe Beau—which, fair. He hadn't exactly seen Beau at his best so far.

Quickly draining his mug and gently pushing Trucker off his lap, he stood and followed him. "Cooper, seriously. You've already been way too nice. So just point me toward the sandwich fixings—"

"Coop."

Beau nearly stumbled over his feet with how fast he stopped short. "I'm sorry, what?"

"You can just call me Coop." Head buried in the fridge, *Coop* missed the surprised look on Beau's face.

Nicknames seemed like a friends thing. Were they friends? Maybe Coop just really didn't like the *er* at the end of his name? Maybe he was against multisyllable names on principle?

Maybe Beau was losing his mind…

Coop pulled out a container that turned out to have lasagna leftovers in it, and Beau nearly teared up.

"I love lasagna," he murmured, staring at the dish as Coop plated a large piece and put it in the microwave.

"Good to know." Coop rewrapped the leftovers and put them away. When he turned back to Beau, he stopped, eyes darting over his face. "What's wrong?"

Beau shook his head and rubbed at the back of his neck. "I just… haven't had it in a while. I'm excited."

Coop's eyes narrowed, but he was distracted when the microwave dinged. The cheese was melting onto the plate and smelled like heaven as he turned around, holding it out to Beau.

"Can't cook?" Coop asked, grabbing him a fork and napkin, then nodding toward the living room when Beau would have sat at the tiny kitchen table.

"Hmm? Oh, I'm okay, but Danny didn't eat pasta or dairy." He carefully carried the plate over to the couch and pushed Trucker away when he tried to fall headfirst into the cheesy goodness.

Coop sat at the other end, back against the armrest and legs up on the cushions—though he kept his knees bent so he didn't invade Beau's space—and snapped his fingers to get Trucker to back off. "Why didn't you just make it for yourself? I'm sure he could have managed to feed himself."

Beau shrugged, digging into the deliciousness and trying to ignore how his face was heating up. "He didn't think I should eat it either, and it didn't seem like it was worth the argument."

He slowly chewed, waiting for Coop to ask the inevitable follow-up questions, like why Beau had put up with that or why Danny had felt the need to try and restrict his diet. When the silence stretched out, the food became tasteless in his mouth as he realized Coop didn't have to ask. He'd seen Beau practically naked.

He already knew why Beau's boyfriend had been unhappy with his body.

CHAPTER FOUR

Never in Coop's life had he ever despised someone before he'd even met them.

He wasn't sure how it had happened, but after spending less than an hour with Beau, he sort of wanted to kick this Danny guy's ass. Which was a little weird considering Coop generally didn't care enough about other people's relationships to get so invested.

But there was something about Beau…

He pulled Trucker between the V of his legs and absently petted him as he studied Beau eating the leftover lasagna. The oversized sweatshirt made him look even smaller than he was and added a layer of vulnerability that Coop wasn't sure he could handle. Helping out people in trouble had been his weakness for years until he finally stopped putting himself in positions of getting taken advantage of.

Mainly, he stopped dating or seeing the same men or women twice.

Before his thoughts could get sucked down a hole of past dating mistakes, he decided to distract himself. "What do you do?"

Beau froze, fork halfway to his mouth, and stared at Coop with wide eyes. He couldn't tell if Beau thought he was so much of an ass that he'd never ask about him or if *no one* ever asked Beau about himself.

"Um, I'm an accountant."

Nodding, he straightened his legs a little but made sure they still didn't touch Beau. "Do you like it?"

Again, Beau's gaze met his in surprise. "Yeah, I do," he said slowly, seemingly waiting for Coop to lose interest or change the subject. "Numbers make sense, and I'm good at it."

"My dad always used to be one of those people who would say things like 'it's never work if you love it,'" Coop said, propping his elbow on the back of the couch and leaning his head on his fist, suddenly tired. "I used to argue with him that a job could just be a job, but now I own my own business and love what I do. He found that hilarious."

Beau nodded and slowly chewed another forkful before responding. "I enjoy my job, but I think that has a lot to do with where I work rather than what I spend all day doing."

"Where do you work?" Coop raised a brow, curiosity getting the best of him.

"I work for my dad's company."

"Does he own the firm or something?" He grunted as Trucker rearranged himself and elbowed him in the gut. Catching the smile Beau tried to hide made it less painful for some reason.

"He owns a land development company. I just work in the finance department." Beau shrugged like that was no big deal and kept his eyes on his mostly empty plate.

"That sounds interesting. Are you two close?"

There was that slow, almost hesitant nod again. "Yeah. My mom died when I was little, so it's just been us ever since. We're… really close." Beau chuckled awkwardly. "I know it's lame, but he's basically my best friend."

Coop frowned, trying to catch Beau's sad brown eyes after he set his empty plate on the coffee table and pulling his legs up to wrap his arms around them. "Hey, that's not lame. My dad and I were really close too. I miss him a lot."

Resting the side of his head on his knees, Beau finally met his gaze. "He died?"

"Yeah," Coop said, voice thick with emotion. "About four years ago. Cancer."

"I'm so sorry, Coop," Beau whispered, reaching over slowly and lightly clasping Coop's ankle, giving it a squeeze before letting go.

"Thank you." He wanted to tell Beau he could touch him longer if he wanted to, but that would be dumb as hell. Not only was Beau literally just out of a shitty relationship, but Coop didn't sleep with people like him—sweet, kind, adorable, but one hundred percent the commitment type. "I'm sorry about your mom."

"Thanks. I was only three, so I don't really remember her."

"Still." They sat silently for several moments, and then Coop said, "And loving your family isn't lame. My siblings drive me crazy, but they're also my favorite people in the world."

Beau's smile wasn't huge, but it was better than the sorrow that had been lingering in the corners of his down-turned mouth. "Why do they drive you crazy?"

Coop laughed. "It's more my sister—she keeps trying to set me up, even though I've told her a hundred times I'm not interested in a relationship. But she's one of those people who are ridiculously happy in their marriage and want everyone else to be happy too, you know?"

Beau nodded and smiled wider. Coop wasn't normally so chatty, but he was finding the warm, quiet cabin and Beau's easy presence to be like a spell weaving around him and drawing the words out. The snow was falling outside, but with the windows covered, they never would have known the storm was still raging.

"My brother is more easygoing, but when we all get together, it's like he turns into a ten-year-old again. We were all at my mom's for Christmas last month, and he and I got into it so bad I almost left."

Eyes wide, Beau rearranged himself so he was cross-legged and facing Coop on the couch. Trucker the Traitor immediately scrambled over to lie across Beau's lap instead.

"What were you fighting over?" Beau asked, fingers digging into Trucker's fur and sending his dog straight to heaven.

"I don't even remember," he said, smiling at Beau's unbelieving face. "Really. Brent just pushes my buttons because he's the baby and can practically get away with murder, and he knows it."

"I can't believe you don't even remember what it was about."

Coop chuckled and relaxed against the couch arm behind him. "You don't have siblings, do you?"

Shaking his head, Beau looked down at Trucker with pink cheeks. "No. Always wanted them though. My dad and I are close, but... Growing up, there were times he wasn't around a lot. He's always been a bit of a workaholic."

That saddened Coop. No mom, absent father... who had taken care of Beau when he was growing up?

Then again, who was taking care of him now? Not that asshole, Danny.

"That must have been lonely." Deciding not to ask about his cheating ex and spoil the mood, he pivoted. "Did you spend a lot of time at friends' houses then?"

Beau grimaced. "Um. When I was younger, I had a couple of close friends. By the time I was in high school though, they'd drifted away, and I had a harder time making new ones."

That surprised Coop. If anything, Beau seemed too trusting, and he was definitely nice enough that he should have had a flock of friends around him. "Why's that? You don't seem that shy."

He shrugged and concentrated on petting Trucker's ears for a long moment. Just when Coop was considering letting him off the hook, Beau said softly, "By that time, my dad's company was… doing really well. We moved to a wealthy neighborhood, and I started going to a new school. It was just… hard to trust that people liked me for me and not because of who my dad was."

Coop was beginning to really wonder who the hell Beau's dad was, but now seemed like the worst possible time to ask. "That sucks, man. I'm sorry."

Beau gave a sort of half shrug and a weak smile. "It's fine. I've learned to judge people's intentions pretty well—though, obviously, I didn't do so great with Danny."

"You can't blame yourself for him being a cheating asshole," Coop protested.

"Not for that, no. But I should have known better," Beau insisted, eyes lighting up as he grew more passionate as he spoke. "He worked for my dad and never showed any interest in the first two years I worked there. Then like a year ago, he suddenly comes around and is all charming smiles and flirting and sweet little gifts." Beau snorted, seemingly annoyed with himself more than anything. "So dumb. He's gorgeous, and I'm—" He gestured at himself and made a face, like that explained anything.

Eyes narrowed, Coop sat up a little straighter. "And you're what? Not gorgeous?"

Fair skin burning with embarrassment, Beau said, "Exactly. For some reason, I let my guard down. I think because it wasn't like he needed me to get in good with my dad, so I didn't see what his ulterior motive was, but I think I figured it out. Since I'm not interested in taking over my dad's company, I think Danny was trying to position himself so that he'd be the obvious choice, you know? Explains why he proposed four months ago when I was waffling about moving in together."

Coop held up a hand finally to halt the flow of words coming from Beau's mouth. "I'm sorry, hang on a second. We need to go back."

"Go back?"

"Yes. Explain to me how you're not gorgeous. Jesus, Beau, have you ever looked in a mirror?" Coop shook his head at Beau's shock. "You don't know, do you? Fuck, your face combined with your ass makes you a knockout as far as I'm concerned."

Beau looked away, fingers trembling in Trucker's fur. "You don't have to say that to make me feel better, okay? I know what I look like. I know I'm chubby and my butt's too big and—"

"*Hey,*" Coop said, voice almost harsh, but it got Beau's attention, his head snapping up and shocked gaze meeting Coop's. "Maybe some guys might think that, but there are plenty of us who like the way boys like you are built. Shit, Beau, if we'd met in literally any other way, I'd have already talked you into bed, and we'd be on our second orgasms of the night."

Primal satisfaction filled Coop as he watched Beau's eyes heat and his Adam's apple bob as he swallowed, gaze darting down to Coop's lap as he bit his plump lower lip. The way Coop was sitting combined with his jeans hid his erection from Beau's eyes, but to make his point, he reached down and adjusted himself in an obvious way.

Butt too big—was that even a thing? Coop wanted to tell

Beau that he bet his ass was mesmerizing when it jiggled during a hard fucking.

"And your ass is not too big," he growled, remembering how Beau had looked in his lacy blue panties, the bottom half of his cheeks bared to his eyes. "Not all men like sleeping with twigs."

No, Beau was exactly the kind of guy Coop liked to fuck —lush in every sense of the word. He liked women the exact same way. With his large frame, he didn't see the point in sleeping with someone he'd have to be so careful with he wouldn't be able to relax and enjoy it.

"Okay," Beau finally whispered, his pink lips red with arousal.

Coop bit back a groan at the image that flashed in his head of Beau in nothing but his blue panties, a pair of fishnet stockings, and face done up in makeup. *Fuck*. He needed to go and cool off before he pulled Beau into his arms and did something they'd both regret.

Standing, he didn't bother hiding his hard cock, enjoying the soft gasp Beau let out at the sight. "I'm going to take Trucker out one last time, then we should go to bed."

Stumbling to his feet, Beau was suddenly right in front of him, chest visibly moving with how heavily he was breathing. "Okay," he said, breathless.

Biting back his smile, Coop stepped around Beau and snapped his fingers to get Trucker to follow him to the door. "You can take the bed. I'll sleep on the couch. I'll be in to use the bathroom and grab some sweats, but feel free to go and get comfortable."

Out of the corner of his eye, he saw Beau deflate as he mumbled an affirmative and trudged toward the bedroom.

As much as Coop knew they couldn't do anything about their attraction, he was man enough to admit he liked that Beau wanted him just as much as he wanted Beau.

Back when he used to imagine himself settling down and having a family, Beau was exactly the kind of guy he'd pictured—smart and sweet and sexy as hell. But he'd given up on that dream years ago.

Then again, he thought as he opened the door and grimaced at the cold blast of air as Trucker darted past him, if anyone could make him reconsider his stance on relationships, it'd be Beau and his adorable smiles and sexy panties.

Too bad after the snow was plowed away, Coop would never see him again.

CHAPTER FIVE

Trying to sleep in a strange man's bed—by *himself*—was harder than Beau would have thought.

He flipped over onto his stomach and groaned when he caught sight of the small alarm clock. 2:13 glared at him in bright red, mocking his inability to sleep. No matter how hard he tried, he kept seeing Danny screwing Alexander over and over again every time he closed his eyes. The quiet of the cabin seemed to amplify the sounds in his head as he had to continue to relive Alexander's lusty moans. It was like live porn in his head but in the *worst possible way*.

Huffing, he flopped onto his back again, the bedding getting all twisted around him and exposing his bare arms and legs to the cool air. He'd tried sleeping in the borrowed sweats, but after two hours of tossing and turning, he'd given up and stripped down to his underwear, hoping he'd finally be able to relax once he was in his usual sleeping attire

Nope.

He should put his pants back on. Lying in Coop's bed awake and thinking about Danny and Alexander sleeping together for three months—how many other surfaces in

Beau's apartment had they tainted?—seemed creepier than just innocently sleeping in his underwear.

Oh god. Now he was thinking about Coop and the things he'd said to Beau right before sending him to bed. Alone. Had he really meant them? As gruff as Coop came off, he'd done nothing but take care of Beau since they'd met—offering him dry pants, making him hot cocoa and then food, not to mention turning off Beau's headlights so his battery didn't die.

Jesus. Beau was a damn mess.

No wonder someone as hot and nice as Coop didn't want to sleep with him. Even if he really did find Beau's body attractive, what did Beau have to offer with his train wreck of a life?

"Stupid Danny messed up everything," he muttered, turning on his side and pulling the pillow from the other side down so he could aggressively cuddle it, punching it into shape. Even if he hadn't been over-the-moon in love with Danny, Beau had been prepared to marry his sorry ass. And he would have been faithful, darn it.

Beau had accepted that he'd have a mediocre sex life, but at least he wouldn't be alone ever again.

Squeezing his eyes shut, a tear leaked out. He sounded so pathetic when he put it like that, but what was wrong with wanting someone to come home to or to do the chores Beau hated or to take care of him when he had a bad day?

Apparently, it was more than Danny had been willing to give.

What was saddest was that Beau had known that. He'd known, deep down, that Danny didn't actually love him. Beau had convinced himself that Danny was compromising, like Beau was, with a person he was comfortable with so that he could start building a life with someone. He'd made himself believe that even if he'd never be completely happy, he'd be content, and he wouldn't be alone.

And he'd convinced himself that was the best he could do.

It was almost funny how fast he'd changed his mind about settling for Danny if he didn't focus on the sleeping-with-another-person part. One day he was accepting the life he thought he deserved, and the next, he was completely done with him and his mediocre dick.

He pressed his face into the pillow he was clutching to stifle an exhausted giggle. He'd bet his car that Coop not only had a good dick but knew how to use it.

Sighing, he flopped onto his back again, arms stretched out to the sides. He really, really needed to not think about Coop's dick if he wanted to get any sleep.

After fussing with the blankets for a minute, he finally settled back down and tried to relax and clear his mind. He could do this. He could stop thinking about Alexander's smirking face and Danny's betrayal and Coop's stupid good looks if he just tried hard enough.

He realized he was squeezing his eyes and hands shut when he heard a scratch at the door that shot him up in bed. For a moment, fear gripped his gut, like maybe a wild animal had gotten into the cabin, killed Coop, and was coming for him next.

Then he heard Trucker softly whine and realized exhaustion was making him even more ridiculous than usual.

He jumped out of bed and hurried to the door, practically tiptoeing to avoid the freezing cold floor. Pulling the door open a little, he stumbled back in surprise when Trucker bowled right through the small opening and past him, curling up on the end of the bed by the time Beau turned around.

Tempted as he was to just slip back between the sheets and go back to lying to himself about being able to sleep, he knew for a fact there was a dog bed right at the end of the footboard on the floor.

Five minutes later, he was convinced Trucker wasn't the good, sweet boy he'd thought he was and that he was actually a devil dog. No matter how sternly he whispered or how many times he snapped his fingers, Trucker never even raised his head.

"Trucker, please, I don't want your daddy to be mad at me when he finds your hair all over his bed. Now come on, get down." He grabbed Trucker's collar and gave it the tiniest tug, not wanting to hurt him, but all that did was make him flop onto his side and sigh. "Really? That's how it is? I'm freezing my ass off here, and you have the nerve to act like I'm bothering you?"

"He can be a bit of a brat," a sleep-rough voice said from behind him.

Beau whirled around, nearly tripping over the stupid dog bed in the process but managing to take a few haphazard steps and catch himself on… Coop's bare chest. *Dear god.* He swallowed roughly as saliva pooled in his mouth at the firm, hairy skin under his hands.

All he wanted was to close that six-inch gap between them and sink into Coop's warmth for the rest of the night. He just knew that if he was cuddled up against all of that muscley goodness, he'd sleep like a baby.

"Sorry," he whispered, slowly peeling his fingers off and taking a step back. Of course, once he wasn't distracted by *Coop's* body, all he could think about was Coop seeing his since he was once again standing in front of him in just his lacy underwear.

Face burning, he crossed his arms over his chest and hunched his shoulders as he turned to the side a little, hoping Coop couldn't see his tummy or love handles in the dark room.

"No, I'm sorry," Coop murmured, having not moved at all from just inside the door. "I didn't mean to scare you."

Beau awkwardly waved him off without uncrossing his arms and cleared his throat as he stepped around the dog bed and tried to retreat to the other side of Coop's bed. It seemed like it'd be less weird, somehow, if he could just get back under the blankets and cover himself up.

"It's fine," he said, voice a little higher pitched than normal. He was more aware than ever of how his ass was jiggling as he hurried away. "I was just trying to get Trucker onto his own bed, but he wasn't having it."

"Yeah, the dog bed is more wishful thinking on my part than anything else," Coop said gruffly. When Beau peeked at him over his shoulder as he reached down to grab the covers, he saw Coop was staring at his ass and rubbing at the back of his head, brown hair sticking out adorably. "Sorry if he woke you up."

Beau paused, one knee up on the bed, and considered his options. As much as his self-esteem had taken a hit from Danny's infidelity, there was no mistaking the look on Coop's face. Even in the darkened room, he could plainly see the way Coop watched him: a little predatory but also cautiously, like he wasn't sure how to handle wanting Beau.

He'd felt rejected in the living room earlier, but he hadn't actually put himself out there, had he? Coop had said he would have slept with him if they'd met another way—did he mean if Beau hadn't just broken up with someone or if Beau wasn't stranded and at Coop's mercy?

Probably both. What little Beau knew about Coop pointed to a man who wouldn't want to take advantage of someone in either of those situations, but especially not combined.

But what if Beau wanted to be taken advantage of?

Or, well, not that exactly. But he didn't want to continue

to lie in Coop's big, warm bed feeling sorry for himself. He wanted to feel wanted, like even though Danny had slept with someone else, Beau was still desirable to someone as hot as Coop.

Fuck, he was scared.

"He… he didn't wake me up," he finally said, lowering his leg back to the ground but keeping his body somewhat averted. He couldn't handle looking Coop square on and striking out. "I couldn't sleep." He took a deep breath and blurted out before Coop could say anything, "Will you stay in here with me?"

Dead silence filled the room for several long moments, and Beau cringed, turning his face completely away from Coop after it felt like an eternity had passed.

"Beau," Coop started, his voice hesitant.

"It's fine," he said quickly, climbing into the bed and practically hiding under the covers he pulled them up so high. "I didn't mean to pressure you."

Coop barked out a harsh chuckle. "I'm not the one being pressured. Beau, if I get in that bed with you, I don't know if I could keep my hands to myself. The last thing you need after the day you had is some guy pawing at you because you're heartbroken and don't want to be alone."

Beau stared at him with his mouth gaping open in what he was sure was a *very* attractive way. He wasn't sure what to say, how to respond to something so thoughtful yet so wrong. Finally, he said absently, "I'm not heartbroken."

"What?" Coop straightened. "What do you mean? Do you want to try and make it work with that asshole?"

That made Beau laugh. "God, no. But I wasn't… We weren't in love, okay?"

Coop shook his head and ran a hand through his shaggy hair. "I don't understand. I thought you said he was your fiancé."

The last thing he wanted was to explain how pathetic he was to Coop—that would have the opposite effect, making Coop pity him, not want to sleep with him.

"He was, but... Look, can we talk about this in the morning? If you don't want to sleep with me, that's fine. But don't use that as an excuse. Danny and I were... We never should have gotten engaged to begin with, and I'm more mad at myself than upset that we're over." Wow, okay, so he'd just spewed a lot of info at Coop.

Again, Coop didn't say anything right away, but Beau didn't know if that was good or bad. Was he thinking about saying yes or trying to come up with a way to turn Beau down that didn't make things awkward for however long they were stuck together in this cabin? Oh shit, why hadn't Beau thought of that before opening his big mouth? Either way, things were going to be weird in the morning between them now. Whether Coop said no or they slept together, they'd have to get through a terrible morning after now because of Beau's big mouth.

He wasn't sure what would be worse, but he did know that even if he couldn't look Coop in the face afterward, he still wanted him to screw his brains out and make him forget—at least for tonight—the scene he'd walked in on. Maybe that was asking a lot from a guy who didn't do any kind of commitments, but it wasn't like Beau was asking him to step into the role of fiancé or something weird like that.

He just wanted to know what it would feel like to be... fucked. Wildly. Passionately. He wanted to feel sore and well-used come morning. As a sort of finale on the last year of his life.

Then, he'd figure out how to start over.

CHAPTER SIX

Coop was so conflicted he was frozen in place.

Even if Beau hadn't been in love with his fiancé—which, what the hell? Beau was so adorably awkward and sweet, why was he settling for some bullshit cheater?—there was no way he wasn't feeling vulnerable.

But he was a grown-ass adult, so who was Coop to tell him he didn't want what he said he wanted? Maybe feeling desirable would help Beau get over the sting of betrayal. Maybe he just needed to feel like he was getting back at Danny by sleeping with someone else too.

Or maybe Coop was looking for an excuse to say yes.

Because, fuck, did he want to.

He wanted to crawl into bed next to Beau, palm his thick ass, and make him scream like Danny the Douche never had.

But what would happen in the morning? Would Beau expect something from Coop he just couldn't give him? They'd probably be snowed in together until Monday at least since it usually took a couple of days after heavy snow for the plows to reach the back road his cabin was on. That would feel like a long time if they were stuck in a tiny space and one of them was upset.

Even knowing that… he couldn't say no.

He took one step forward and heard Beau suck in a breath, his soft body hidden under the covers and only his sweet, pale face peeking out over them. "Are you sure?" Coop asked, because he had to. He had to know they were both one hundred percent on board.

Beau nodded quickly, his bed-tousled hair flopping around in the most adorable way.

Coop nodded too, then snapped his fingers at Trucker, pointing toward the open door. "Sorry, buddy," he said as his dog jumped down with a huff, "you're getting sexiled."

The little giggle from Beau made him smile as he shut the door firmly behind Trucker. Once he was sure his sneaky dog couldn't climb back into bed with them while he was balls-deep inside Beau, he turned and strode forward. Only to stutter to a stop as his brain caught up to what he was thinking.

"Do you have a condom?" He had to bite back a smile when he flicked on the bedside lamp and caught Beau's pink face and wide eyes. "I don't bring anything but lube with me because I'm always alone when I come up here."

A look he couldn't quite identify shadowed Beau's beautiful, brown eyes, but it flickered away as fast as it had appeared. "Um, maybe in with my toiletries. I'm not sure."

Right, because he'd been so distraught over finding his fiancé fucking someone else, he'd literally forgotten to pack pants. Why would he remember if he had a spare condom rolling around somewhere?

When Beau didn't get up, Coop raised his eyebrows and pressed his lips together to stop from grinning. How someone as gorgeous, sweet, and *self-conscious* as Beau had crashed into Coop's life and just talked him into bed was beyond him. "Were you going to go look? We don't have to fuck if you don't want to or don't like that."

That seemed to draw Beau up short. "What else would we do?"

Coop couldn't decide if he was pissed that all of Beau's partners had been selfish assholes or if he found the way Beau was staring up at him almost innocently adorable as hell. "Anything we want, sweetheart."

Fuck, he hadn't meant to say that. Endearments were something couples did, not onetime hookups. But the deepening of the flush in Beau's cheeks and the dilating of his pupils said he liked it a lot, and god damn but Coop was helpless against that look.

Making up his mind, Coop studied Beau's face as he tucked his thumbs into the waistband of his sweats and slowly started to inch them down. Pride filled his chest as the base of his hard cock came into view and Beau licked his damn lips, sitting up a little for a better view. The rest of his erection was clearly outlined, pointed down toward his left leg, the only thing holding it in place the soft gray material of his pants.

So, so slowly, he kept pushing them down until his cock sprang free, the wide head already damp with precum and shaft slightly curved.

He knew he had nothing to worry about, size- or width-wise, but he still smirked at the choked-back groan Beau let out as he stared at Coop's cock.

Shit, he was so hungry for it. Coop couldn't wait to feed it to him.

He let his sweats drop to the floor, grabbed the bottle of lube out of the nightstand, and started climbing up onto the bed.

"Wait."

Freezing, he wondered for a second if Beau had changed

his mind, and his stomach dropped. As much as he'd waffled on whether it was a good idea or not, now that he'd decided to go for it, he'd be disappointed if he didn't get to touch Beau's beautifully lush body.

"What's wrong?"

"You forgot to turn off the light," Beau said, gripping the edge of the covers tightly, like Coop hadn't already seen nearly every single inch of him. Like the sight of him in his sexy little panties wasn't burned into his brain forever.

"Sweetheart, if you really want me to, I'll turn it off, but I'd love to be able to see you. I *want* to see you falling apart under my hands… and tongue." Fuck, did he have plans for his tongue. Even if his cock didn't end up in Beau's ass, that didn't mean he wasn't going to enjoy the hell out of it.

Audibly swallowing, Beau held his gaze for a long moment, but Coop was so fucking proud of him when he finally nodded a little and whispered, "Okay. You can leave it on."

Grinning, he peeled back the covers, gently tugging them out of Beau's grip and baring his gorgeous body to Coop's eyes. As nervous as he was, Beau's cock was hard and straining against the lacy blue fabric covering them, a wet spot darkening the material right over the tip.

He was about to dive in, already practically able to taste Beau's salty precum, but when he glanced up and caught Beau chewing nervously on his lower lip, he paused and changed course. Settling carefully over Beau's body, he frowned at the faint trembling he could feel now that they were pressed together.

"Are you okay?" He nudged his nose against the underside of Beau's jaw, encouraging him to bare his neck so he could lay a few kisses down the pale column.

Beau shivered and nodded, bumping into Coop's head

with his chin. "Yeah, just a little nervous and cold. Though you're warming me up nicely."

Chuckling, he nipped at Beau's Adam's apple before slowly moving up to the point of his chin, pressing tiny kisses over the slightly rough skin. He didn't have what technically qualified as a five-o'clock shadow, but there was just enough stubble to feel abrasive against Coop's lips.

When he reached Beau's chin, he paused, caught in his luminous gaze. Coop didn't usually kiss his hookups—kissing was intimate in a way he didn't want to be. It was already hard enough to try and keep Beau in the box with other people he'd slept with in recent years—the one marked *No Strings Attached.* But one look at the tip of Beau's tongue peeking out to swipe against his bottom lip and Coop was done.

God damn, he was breaking all of his rules for Beau Singer.

He started by tracing that same path with his own tongue, intending on kissing Beau soft and sweet like he deserved, but when Beau groaned roughly and gripped at Coop's shoulders desperately, Coop couldn't hold back. He sank into Beau's mouth like a cool bath on a scorching hot day, savoring his first taste and already greedy for more.

Beau's nails digging into his skin was just this side of painful, grounding him to the moment so he didn't float away on the feeling of Beau's soft lips and shy tongue. With a last little nibble on Beau's bottom lip, he broke away to catch his breath. He couldn't help but feel smug at the surprised look on his face.

"Feeling warmer?" he couldn't help but ask, happiness bubbling up inside him when Beau laughed softly and gave his shoulder a whack.

"Much," he murmured, then leaned up and gently kissed Coop once more before falling back onto the bed. For some reason, that gentle press of lips combined with the warm feeling growing in his chest left Coop feeling disoriented and a little shaken.

"Good," he said, voice a little gruff, but it only made Beau smile wider for some reason. "Want you to feel good."

He ducked down and started kissing across Beau's chest before he could respond. Why was he being so weird? He needed to treat Beau like anyone else—make sure he was satisfied but keep things impersonal.

His brilliant plan lasted about thirty seconds.

As he sucked on one of Beau's nipples and pinched the other, Beau cried out and arched against him, fingers sinking into Coop's hair and holding him tightly. He grunted at the slight sting but didn't let up, flicking his tongue over the small nub over and over, feeling drunk on power as Beau's voice got higher and breathier.

"Oh god, oh god, oh god." Beau spread his legs so Coop was cradled between his hips, then thrust upward, his lace-covered cock rubbing against Coop's abdomen. "Oh god, that feels so good."

"You like how your lacy panties feel on your cock?" he murmured against Beau's chest, biting and sucking on a patch of skin on his soft pec.

Beau was gasping already, his body strung tight like he was feeling things he'd never felt before, and a not-small part of Coop hoped that was true. That he'd make Beau feel so good, so sexy, he'd never settle for some asshole like Danny the Douche again.

"*Yes,*" Beau panted out, legs restless against the sheet beneath him. "It's almost a little rough against my skin, but I love it."

Jesus. His sweet little accountant liked how rough the lace felt against his hard cock? Coop was going to combust if he wasn't careful.

Groaning, he kissed his way down Beau's body, ready to taste that precum-soaked fabric. He ignored how Beau sucked in his stomach, simply laying a few extra kisses around his belly button, then moving on. He nearly swallowed his tongue when he got to Beau's groin and saw how his cock was pushing the sexy panties away from his body. He ran his tongue over the edge right where it was digging into his hip. Resisting the urge to give his little love handle a bite, he snagged the waistband of the underwear with his teeth, pulled on it, then let it go so it snapped back against his skin.

Beau's back arched so beautiful as he cried out, Coop nearly did it again, but the scent of Beau's precum was too tantalizing. He ran his tongue over the lace from the base of Beau's cock all the way to the soaking wet patch over the head. As he sucked the material into his mouth and ran his tongue over the roughness, he groaned at the exploding flavor of Beau.

It wasn't enough.

Nearly frantic with need, he sat up onto his knees and grabbed at the panties, pulling at them to lower them and expose Beau. He froze at the telltale sound of tearing fabric.

"Fuck. I'm so sorry—"

"Don't care," Beau interrupted, head thrashing back and forth and hands fisting into the sheet beneath him. "Get them off. I have more."

Sucking in a breath so hard his nostrils flared, he pinpointed the seam over Beau's right hip where it had already begun to tear and pulled. The gasping cry Beau let out as Coop literally tore his underwear from his body would stay with Coop for the rest of his life, he was sure of it. Quickly ripping the other side, he pulled the fabric away from Beau's body but paused before throwing them aside, raising them to his face for one last rub against his bearded cheek, inhaling the salty scent of Beau's arousal.

"Jesus Christ, Coop," Beau said, staring at his panties like he'd never seen them before, chocolatey-brown eyes little more than pupil. His chest heaved as he tried to catch his breath.

With a grin, Coop tossed the torn fabric away, making sure they landed behind the chair in the corner of the room. No matter what the weekend brought, he knew he was keeping those as a reminder of the sexy man who'd befriended his dog and tore down the walls Coop had been building for years in a matter of hours.

Then again, if they'd come down so easily, how well built had they really been?

CHAPTER SEVEN

Beau was on fire.

In the back of his head, he was a little embarrassed at how he was moaning and thrashing around, but mostly he didn't care. The way Coop touched him and talked to him drove him out of his mind. There was nothing he wanted more than for Coop to make him come.

Nothing else mattered.

Even though he was laid out naked in front of a gorgeous lumberjack of a man, Beau still couldn't bring himself to really mind. Not anymore. Not when Coop was looking at him with heat in his dark blue eyes and doing things like smelling Beau's arousal on his panties.

God damn, why was that so hot?

Coop leaned over him, bracing both arms on the bed by Beau's head, and planted a deep, tongue-thrusting kiss on his mouth, swallowing his whimpers. He palmed the thick muscles running down Coop's wide back and sank into the sensations coursing through him. Coop's beard was abrading his skin but in a way that made him want to feel it over every inch of his body. For the first time in a long time, he felt small and delicate. Compared to Coop's muscles and large frame, he was practically tiny. He'd carried extra weight around his midsection, ass, and thighs for years and usually felt… cumbersome compared to his partners, despite being so short.

But as Coop twisted one of his big hands into Beau's hair and tugged his head back farther, taking everything Beau had to give and leaving him melted into a pile of goo with a damn kiss, Beau couldn't feel anything but desirable.

Pulling away, Coop stared down at Beau for a long second, eyes roaming over Beau's face and lingering on his lips. "You kiss like…"

"What?" Beau whispered, worried he'd done something wrong. Danny had never complained about how he'd kissed, but what if that was part of why he'd turned to Alexander for sex? Could Beau's kisses be that disgusting? Oh god, he was a terrible—

"Hey, where'd you go?" Coop whispered, deep voice just coarse enough to cut through his panic and bring him back from the edge.

"I'm here," he croaked, tightening his grip on Coop's torso. "What do I kiss like?"

Eyes narrowing, it looked like Coop was going to press for more, but then he just dipped down and nuzzled the side of Beau's face, making him gasp at the rough scrape, and his heart tripped in his freaking chest. "Like if I stop, you'll die."

Beau groaned theatrically but then couldn't help but giggle. Sounded about accurate. "It's your fault for being so good at it."

Coop laughed softly, the warm air hitting Beau's neck and making him shiver. "Well, I'm not sorry. I don't know if I'll ever get enough of your mouth."

Beau's breath caught in the back of his throat, and he couldn't help but clench his arms around Coop's shoulders a little harder. God, he wanted that. Wanted Coop to desire him for more than a night or a weekend.

Wanted someone as good and decent as Coop to crave him for the rest of their life.

Coop, not knowing he'd just sent Beau's mind spinning into the stratosphere, sucked a hickey onto his neck that made his toes curl, then gently pulled out of Beau's hold so he was kneeling between his legs once more. "I definitely want to kiss more of your body though."

Biting his lip, Beau slowly slid his feet up, raising his knees and spreading his legs. His heart was beating in his throat so hard he couldn't say anything, but judging by Coop's soft groan and the way he licked his lower lip, he was okay with that.

"So sexy," Coop murmured, eyes running over Beau's thighs and cock and up to his chest before locking with Beau's once more. "Is there anything you really want? Or anything you don't like?"

What a question. Beau licked his lips, mind racing with possibilities, but he couldn't come up with a single thing he didn't think he'd like if Coop was the one doing it. "Um, can I… suck you?"

The smile Coop gave him was downright *filthy*. "Yeah, sweetheart. I'd really like that."

Coop settled against the headboard, legs splayed out shamelessly, and Beau gave himself a little pep talk as he eyed the size of Coop's erection. *You got this.* When he knelt between Coop's legs, he nearly swallowed his tongue at the way Coop was stroking himself as he waited for Beau to get it together.

"You're a lot bigger than Danny was," he blurted out, then felt his face start to burn as he flushed. Why had he said that? God.

Coop smiled but didn't stop moving his hand, the sight of

his fat head reappearing above his fist over and over hypnotic. "Are you worried? You can change your mind if you don't want to do this anymore."

"I do," he quickly said, nodding and scooting closer, laying his hands on Coop's well-muscled thighs and sliding up slowly until he was framing Coop's pelvis. "I want to."

"Okay," Coop said quietly. After one more stroke, he stopped with his fist just below the head and waited, holding himself out to Beau like an offering.

Watching a pearly drop of precum bead up and slide over the wide crown, landing on Coop's callused fingers, was pornographic. Moaning, he dropped onto his belly gracelessly and dove forward, mouth open and tongue out. As soon as Coop's essence hit his taste buds, he moaned again and closed his lips to suckle more of the flavor into his mouth.

Coop grunted as his hand dropped away. "Jesus. Yeah, just like that, sweetheart."

Feeling emboldened, Beau sucked harder, running his tongue along the dips and ridges. He used one hand to squeeze the thick base, then stroked up to meet his mouth, letting the mixture of precum and spit leaking past his lips smooth the way.

Coop kept groaning, a hand coming up to tangle in Beau's hair and encourage him to start bobbing his head, taking in as much as he could. Beau followed the gentle, unspoken instructions and sped up his movements, growing frantic with his need to see Coop explode.

When he went too far down and gagged a little, Coop hissed and tightened his hold, his whole body growing taut. "Fuck yeah. You're okay."

Coop's fingers unclenched in Beau's hair, and he pulled back so only the head was in his mouth, resting on his tongue, and tried to catch his breath.

"You want to make me come?" Coop rasped, running his hand over Beau's head and through his hair, practically making him purr.

"Uh-huh." He nodded slowly, sucking on Coop's head as he met his fiery gaze.

"So fucking sexy." Coop gripped the back of his neck and pulled Beau up his body, slamming their mouths together in a wet kiss. When Beau had to rip away so he could breathe, Coop grinned and guided him back down to his dick with a hand on his shoulder. "Do it then. Make me come."

He dove back in, running his tongue up and down Coop's shaft, sucking his balls into his mouth, then returning to his sensitive head. Stroking and licking and sucking. Everything was wet. The slurping sounds were so loud in the quiet room it was obscene, and Beau was *reveling* in how Coop kept groaning, Coop's low, encouraging words driving Beau to suck harder and stroke faster.

When he could tell Coop was getting close, his thighs clenching tight on either side of him and his words shifting to little more than guttural grunts, Beau bobbed his head a few more times. Sucking in a breath through his nose, he went down once more but kept going until he gagged himself again, remembering how much Coop had liked it the first time.

Sure enough, Coop swelled and exploded before Beau could pull up, causing him to sputter and cough a little, but he did his best to keep stroking Coop's shaft and suck down every last drop.

"Too much," Coop finally murmured.

Beau pulled off and sat up on his knees, wiping at his wet face and grinning triumphantly. "Good?"

"Jesus. How can you ask that? I'm practically boneless, sweetheart."

More than a little pleased with himself, he started to

crawl forward, intent on cuddling up next to Coop and uncaring that his own erection was still throbbing, but Coop stopped him.

"Don't move," Coop growled while Beau was still on his hands and knees. Coop slid out from under him and crowded up behind him, palming his ass cheeks. "Perfection. Get down on your elbows. I want this ass in the air, sweetheart."

Embarrassed and more aroused than he'd ever been, Beau dropped to his forearms and buried his head between them. When Coop's big, rough hands spread him apart, he thought he'd die. A whimpering meep escaped his mouth, and Coop chuckled, breath brushing the exposed skin between his cheeks.

"You like getting rimmed?" Coop asked, brushing his beard down his crack and laughing again when Beau moaned. "So sensitive."

"I've never been… um, rimmed," Beau whispered.

Coop's fingers tightened on his cheeks, but all he said was, "I bet you'll love it. Your ass was made for worshipping."

Releasing a choked groan, he pushed his face farther into the bed under him.

Then Coop's warm, wet tongue ran from just behind his balls to his hole, and he gasped.

"Mmhmm. If it's too much, just tell me to stop, okay?"

Beau had barely nodded before Coop had his face buried between his cheeks, beard and tongue both teasing him relentlessly.

"Oh god," he moaned when Coop wiggled the tip of his tongue right at Beau's entrance, lightning shooting through his limbs. Arching his back, he gave in to what he wanted and forced himself to forget how embarrassed he'd felt at being so exposed. "More, please."

Coop grunted an acknowledgment and kept working his

way inside Beau's body using only his lips and tongue and teeth. Feeling like a live wire, Beau screamed into the mattress when Coop suddenly scraped his chin up across his hole.

"Oh god, your beard," he panted out, body feeling loose and coiled tight all at the same time.

"Good?"

"So good."

Coop chuckled and nipped each of Beau's cheeks before doing it again. Beau couldn't help but cry out once more, the sensation almost too much but still something he craved to feel over and over. When Coop's tongue wiggled inside him finally, he gasped and shot a hand down to grip his base so he didn't come. He didn't want it to be over yet. He needed more.

He'd never felt so greedy.

Coop thrust his tongue into Beau repeatedly, fingers digging into his cheeks. It was all too much, and he wondered if he'd ever be satisfied with mediocre sex again.

"Stroke yourself, Beau. I wanna feel you clench down on my tongue as you come," Coop rasped against his spit-wet skin.

Whole body shaking and muscles strung so tight he thought he'd break into a million pieces at any moment, he turned his head so he didn't suffocate on the bunched-up sheet under him. His hand flew on his shaft as Coop pressed his tongue back inside.

"Ungh, ungh, ungh," he grunted as his body strained, reaching for that explosion just out of reach. Just when he thought he wouldn't get there, that he'd plateaued and would be forced to stay rock hard all night, Coop slipped a hand down and gave Beau's balls a squeeze. The shot of painful pleasure was exactly what he needed, stars erupting behind his eyes as he cried out and came.

He was breathing like he'd run a marathon as Coop slowly withdrew his tongue, pressing a kiss to Beau's sensitive hole and stroking his aching balls. His other hand petted Beau from butt to shoulder blades like he was trying to gentle a wild animal.

When he started to move, Coop's big, gentle hands were there to help ease him onto his back. "I'm going to grab a washcloth," he said. "Don't move."

Beau chuckled weakly. "Not a problem. I don't think I'll ever be able to move again."

Coop's grin was smug as hell as he climbed off the bed and disappeared into the bathroom. Time didn't seem to mean anything anymore. It seemed like Beau only blinked his eyes, and Coop was back in bed, running a warm cloth over his groin and belly. He didn't even have the energy to be embarrassed at Coop touching his soft midsection.

He blinked again, and they were under the blankets, Coop gently pulling him into his arms and pressing a quick, minty kiss to his lips.

The last thought Beau had before he finally fell asleep, body tingly and sated, was that he'd been wrong. Phenomenal, earth-shattering sex was a real thing.

Now he just had to figure out how he'd survive never getting to experience it again.

CHAPTER EIGHT

Coop had a problem, and its name was Beau Singer.

Sighing, Coop trudged through the foot and a half of snow that had fallen the night before and followed Trucker as he took off behind the cabin and into the woods. Trucker had been practically busting the bedroom door down twenty minutes ago, and Coop wasn't sure how Beau had slept through it.

Then again, he'd been pretty tuckered out last night, practically passing out as soon as he came.

Coop grinned up at the clear, perfectly blue sky, ignoring his thickening cock as he remembered how sweet Beau had moaned when Coop had eaten his ass and rubbed his beard between his cheeks.

Fuck, he could spend *days* feasting on that man's ass.

And that was part of the problem. He followed the tracks Trucker had left for him and headed off again, sucking the biting cold into his lungs and trying to find that peaceful feeling in his chest he always had when he was at his cabin. But it was gone.

It wasn't that Beau was disturbing his tranquil week in

the woods. He knew himself well enough to know that wasn't what had been brewing in the back of his head ever since he'd woken up.

It was that Beau made him *want things*. Things that he had no business wanting anymore. He'd tried the whole relationship thing too many times to count. Had been dumped, cheated on, stolen from, and dumped again. The final straw had been about five years ago when his boyfriend of two years—who Coop had planned on fucking spending the rest of his life with—had emptied Coop's bank account and run off with his yoga instructor or some shit.

As Trucker came into view once more, half carrying and half dragging a damn tree branch, Coop huffed out a breath and tried to relax his shoulders. He'd adopted Trucker about six months after that last failed relationship and sworn off boyfriends and girlfriends.

The two of them had been perfectly content together ever since.

But what if Beau could make him more than content? What if he could bring laughter back into Coop's life?

He eyed the "stick" his dog dropped at his feet and chuckled. Then again, his dog did some crazy antics—who needed a sweet man with a thick ass to make him happy?

You do, dumbass, the voice in his head said, and it sounded a lot like his sister. Which was disturbing on a lot of levels.

Grunting, he shook his head at his dog, gave him a rub around his ears, then turned and headed off in another direction. Trucker abandoned the branch and bounded after him, searching for another stick or a rabbit to chase.

The problem with falling for Beau—not that he was because he'd known the man less than a day for god's sake—was that Coop knew going in that it wouldn't work out. Their expiration date was written on the snow-covered road in front of his house. Once it was clear and Beau could either head back home or on to his dad's cabin, Coop had zero doubts that he would. Even if he didn't leave immediately, it wasn't like they could both stay here, cut off from the real world and all their responsibilities, for the rest of their lives.

No matter how he looked at it, sleeping with Beau had been a terrible idea, but he couldn't actually regret it. Not when Beau had been so honest and open with him—in and out of bed—and come alive under his hands.

But he absolutely couldn't do it again.

He made it less than twelve hours.

All day he and Beau had been fine around each other. When Coop had come back from walking Trucker, Beau had been awake and dressed in another pair of Coop's sweats, apologizing for taking them without permission and blushing.

It had been too fucking cute.

They'd eaten breakfast, Beau had talked to his dad—that had been an *interesting* conversation to eavesdrop on—and then they'd mostly just hung out all day. There wasn't any internet, and the TV only got basic cable from an antenna that was hit-or-miss on a good day. But that was what Coop liked about it. He'd thought about going ice fishing so they weren't in each other's space all day but had known Beau would see it as Coop avoiding him. Would probably think Coop regretted the night before or something ridiculous like that.

So he'd pulled out one of the books he'd brought with him and relaxed on the couch, Beau curled up in the large recliner playing on his phone, then stealing the other book when he apparently got bored of scrolling.

They were just finishing cleaning up their dinner dishes when it happened.

"Do you have any movies we could watch?" Beau asked, meticulously drying the plate in his hands, Trucker pressed against his legs.

It was an innocent enough question, but the answer wasn't. "Um, not really."

"Oh." Beau seemed to deem the dish dry enough, placing it in the cupboard, then folded the towel he was using and hung it over the oven handle. "Does that mean only like a couple crappy ones or none at all? Because I'm so bored I'll watch anything. I don't know how you read mysteries."

"You could download something else to read on your phone, you know," Coop pointed out, carefully ignoring his question.

"Yeah, I guess," Beau said, shuffling off into the living room, shoulders a little dejected-looking.

Coop sighed and followed. "The only DVDs I have here are porn, okay?"

That brought Beau up short, his socked feet literally sliding on the floor as he tried to stop and turn around at the same time. "*What*?"

He couldn't help but smirk at Beau's pink cheeks. "Porn, as in pornography. As in videos of two or more people—"

"Okay!" Beau hastily interrupted, blushing harder at Coop's chuckles. "I didn't… even know you could still buy porn that way."

Coop shrugged and lowered himself onto the couch, feet stretched out across the cushions and Trucker jumping up on the other end. He reached for his paperback on the coffee table. "I don't watch a lot of TV anyway, but not being able to stream porn when I'm here for a week or two can be annoying."

Beau stared at him. His mouth was slightly parted, and he

had a hand on the back of the recliner like he had to hold himself up because he was so offended by the idea of someone regularly watching pornography. When he dropped his eyes to Beau's groin, he realized it wasn't outrage Beau was feeling.

They stared at each other, the room filling with a delicious tension. Coop knew he should change the subject, go back to his book, and put the conversation behind him.

But Beau wasn't wearing any fucking underwear under Coop's gray sweats, so he couldn't be responsible for what he did next.

"You want to watch one?"

The question seemed to surprise Beau, his whole body jolting like Coop had goosed him. "Oh, um… what are they about?"

Raising a brow, Coop stared at him. "You mean the shitty plots they try and include or the positions the actors do in them?"

Beau's Adam's apple bobbed as he swallowed roughly, biting at his lower lip in a way that made Coop's dick take notice. "The s-second one."

He grinned and held Beau's gaze as he said, "Well, one has a really hot threesome scene where one of the guys gets DPed and another—"

"What's that?" Beau asked, his legs finally giving out as he sort of collapsed onto the recliner, eyes wide.

"DP? It's double penetration. Where one guy takes two dicks or a dick and dildo into his ass at the same time."

Beau gasped, one hand flying up to cover his mouth. He didn't look scared though, and that forced Coop to have to rearrange his dick in his jeans before he lost circulation. Beau watched his movements, hand sliding down to rest at the base of his throat.

"What else?"

Jesus. Coop sat up and leaned forward onto his thighs, forgotten book landing between his knees. "Another one has a spanking scene that's pretty hot." Beau's nose crinkled. *Okay, not a fan of spankings.* "The threesome scene also has a great spit-roasting of the same guy who took the two dicks."

Beau swallowed hard, but a pensive frown tugged at the corner of his mouth. "What's that?"

"I feel like I'm corrupting you." He couldn't help but smile though.

Eyes rolling, Beau leaned back and crossed his arms, but the obvious hard-on in his sweats negated the effect considerably. "More like teaching me things I probably should have learned in college."

"Well, I don't know where you went to school, but they probably didn't offer classes on spit-roasting or double penetration."

"You know what I mean," Beau said, giggling even as his face got redder. "I didn't really date as a freshman or sophomore, then dated the same guy for most of junior and all of senior year."

"Seems like there's a story there." He didn't want to push for more if the relationship had ended badly, but something in Beau's vulnerable eyes and open face just drew him in every single time. Their conversation had clearly been headed toward a repeat of the night before, and then suddenly, they were talking about another one of Beau's exes.

How the hell had that happened?

"Not really." Beau shrugged. "He was studying accounting too, and I thought we were well matched, but... Right before graduation, he broke up with me and told me he was moving to Florida to work for his uncle's friend or something."

Coop waited, expecting Beau to continue. When he didn't, he prompted, "You didn't want to go with him?"

Beau cleared his throat and looked away. "He didn't ask

me to go with him. When I started to tell him that I didn't think I could leave my dad, he told me… Well, he made it clear he didn't want me to go with him."

By saying something hurtful. Coop filled in the rest. Sneering, he said, "His fucking loss. He should have begged you to move with him."

Even as the words were coming out of his mouth, Coop wanted to stop them. The last thing he wanted was to inadvertently lead Beau on or give him the idea that Beau should ask Coop to move closer to him or something crazy like that. One night of fantastic sex was not the beginning of an epic romance.

Even if it was followed by a day of relaxing silence that would have driven most men crazy, but Beau seemed to understand and accept that Coop wasn't the type to talk all day.

Not to mention how Beau had snuck little bites of food to Trucker under the table when he thought Coop wasn't looking. Or the simple fact that Trucker had fallen in love with Beau immediately and might actually prefer him to Coop.

And he definitely wasn't going to think about how Beau's nose crinkled when he laughed or how his cheeks flushed pink when he was aroused or how his ass jiggled under his borrowed sweats when he ran after Trucker when the dog tried to bring a stick inside after Beau played with him that afternoon for nearly forty minutes.

Luckily, Beau just smiled weakly at him and changed the subject. Though he changed it back to porn, and Coop was now more convinced than ever that they shouldn't sleep together again. One more mind-melting orgasm, and Coop might be the one asking Beau to move.

"So what's spit-roasting?" Beau stumbled over the words but tried to look confident, straightening his shoulders.

Coop grinned slowly and held Beau's gaze. "It's where

one man's fucking your mouth and another your ass at the same time."

Mouth dropping open, Beau just stared at him for a moment. Coop carefully watched how his chest rose and fell a little faster.

"Have you ever..." Even though Beau didn't finish his question, it wasn't hard for Coop to guess where he was going with it.

"Had a threesome?"

Beau silently nodded, bright gaze unwavering.

Coop shrugged. "Not since college. I found out quickly I'm not into sharing."

Which was true and not true. It was true in that he didn't share his partners when they were in a relationship, but if one of the people he'd hooked up with over the last few years had suggested a threesome? He probably would have said yes. He liked sex, and he'd done a great job of keeping his heart uninvolved.

Until now.

Coop waited for Beau to collect his thoughts, which he could see whirling in his brain from where he was sitting. He expected Beau to suggest they watch one of the DVDs or for Beau to slip over onto the couch. He was expecting to have to make the first move if things were to actually progress to sex.

He damn sure wasn't expecting Beau to slowly climb to his feet and stick one of his hands into his pocket, pulling something out and holding it up between his fingers. It took a moment for Coop to realize what he was looking at, but as soon as he did, arousal shot through him so fast he got light-headed for a second.

"I found this in my shaving kit," Beau whispered, condom wrapper catching the light as his fingers trembled just a little. "Wanna use it?"

CHAPTER NINE

Standing in front of Coop holding that condom was possibly the scariest thing Beau had ever done.

But he also kind of loved it.

His heart was racing and his palms were sweaty and he'd never felt more alive.

If they hadn't already messed around the night before, Beau never would have had the courage to suggest they have sex. But they had, and it had been awesome. Even though they hadn't talked about it at all after waking up, Coop's eyes had crinkled in a soft smile when he'd handed Beau a mug full of steaming coffee that morning. It had been just after he'd returned from taking Trucker out first thing, and Beau had known everything was fine between them.

And that was supposed to be it. One and done and then never see each other again after Beau got his car out of the driveway.

But when he'd seen that condom in his shaving kit when he'd gone to shower, the idea of using it had taken root in the back of his brain and grown to a damn beanstalk by the time Coop was grunting in response as Beau chattered while they ate dinner. He'd known that Coop was listening even if his responses were mostly noises and not so much words because when Beau told a funny story about the dog he'd had growing up, Coop chuckled and smiled in appreciation, casting a fond glance at where Trucker had been sitting next to Beau.

How often had Danny rolled his eyes and told Beau he was being too loud, that Danny liked to decompress in silence after work? Beau didn't feel like he was overly chatty, but he did like to share his day with someone, complaining about a coworker or raving about the new place he'd gone to for lunch. Whereas Danny had never wanted to talk about important things. Preferring to wind down in front of the TV or on his computer in his office after dinner.

Beau knew that Coop had liked the soft quiet they'd shared for most of the day, but it had also been obvious he didn't mind Beau sharing random tidbits while they ate, and that had been the deciding factor for Beau.

Was it kind of sad that he'd decided to sleep with a guy because he didn't get annoyed at his voice? He mentally shrugged and held on to his smile, despite it taking longer than he'd thought for Coop to respond to his proposition.

What if he said no?

Just when Beau was about to start second-guessing the entire idea, Coop slowly stood, setting his book on the table and stepping around it so he was within reach. Beau had to tip his head back to keep holding his gaze, Coop was so much taller than him. He knew his smile probably looked forced, but Coop's silence was getting to him.

"Coop?"

There was another moment where Coop studied him, eyes darting all over his face. Then he nodded slowly, a small smile breaking his stern face. "You know this is a terrible idea, right?" Coop said, voice soft and gruff.

Beau shrugged as his mind helpfully started pointing out all the other terrible choices Beau had made recently. "What's one more on the list?"

The permanent frown lines between Coop's brows deepened as he shook his head, but his hands came up to frame Beau's face, one of his thumbs brushing across his lips. "I should say no, but after trying to convince myself all day to keep my hands off you, I can't do it anymore."

Beau's heart swelled. It wasn't a declaration or anything, but just the acknowledgment that Coop was craving Beau as much as Beau was him gave him the courage to raise up onto his tiptoes and slot their mouths together. Lips moving slowly, they took their time exploring and relearning the feel and taste of each other. Whereas last night had felt almost frantic, their movements now were languid. There was heat simmering between them, but no sense of urgency.

After several minutes of kissing and softly groping each other, Coop started steering Beau backward toward the bedroom. The moment felt so full of potential, passion practically shimmering in the air.

So, of course, Beau tripped over his own feet halfway to the bed.

The only thing that stopped him from landing on his ass was Coop's strong hold on him. Laughing, Coop pressed his face into the crook of Beau's neck, his whole body shaking.

"Stop laughing!" Beau exclaimed, slapping at his shoulder but unable to hold back his own chuckles.

"Sorry."

He didn't sound sorry at all.

But he did kiss Beau in apology, gently swiping his tongue inside and humming. Beau's annoyance was forgotten as they slowly undressed each other before climbing into bed.

Coop had to jump back up and shoo Trucker out of the

room when he hopped up next to them, sending Beau into another fit of giggles. But when Coop landed on top of him, taking his mouth in a harder kiss, the laughter dried up once more.

For long, heated moments, they did nothing but kiss and run their hands over each other, their cocks brushing together every once in a while. When Beau couldn't take the slow pace anymore, he pulled his swollen mouth away from Coop and whispered, "Get the lube."

The grin Coop threw him before reaching for the lube and abandoned condom on the nightstand was predatory. A shiver raced down Beau's spine as he started to turn onto his stomach.

Coop's callused hand on his shoulder stopped him. "No. Like this."

Beau nodded silently as he settled on his back once more, but a part of him wondered if something had changed between them and he'd missed it. Having Coop make love to him face-to-face seemed way too intimate for a guy not interested in a relationship of any kind.

But he wouldn't pass up the chance to watch Coop's face as he sank inside him.

Wasting no time, Coop lubed up his fingers and pressed one inside. Beau arched off the bed and moaned, wondering how one thick finger could already feel so good when he'd been dissatisfied with Danny's cock for so long. He shook his head, displacing any thoughts of his ex. All he wanted was to focus on Coop and the moment they were sharing. Danny didn't belong anywhere near Coop's bedroom.

By the time Coop was thrusting two fingers inside him, Beau was gasping for breath and clutching at Coop's shoulders. When a third finger tried to press in, he placed a hand on Coop's chest. "I'm ready."

Coop laughed and kept going. "No, you aren't. You still feel so tight, sweetheart."

He tried to frown up at him, but Coop just smirked and pegged his prostate for the first time. Beau's back bowed off the mattress as he cried out.

"That's… cheating."

"My cock is a lot bigger than my fingers," Coop murmured, leaning over to rub their cheeks together. "I refuse to hurt you."

"Let me ride you then," Beau blurted out. As soon as the idea was out in the open, he wanted it. Desperately. It'd been a long time since he'd done it because He-Who-Shall-Not-Be-Named used to complain that Beau was too heavy to be on top. But he remembered loving it. "That way I can control things a bit."

"Okay." Coop thrust his fingers a couple more times, then kissed Beau as he spread them and pulled out of his body. "Sounds like a good idea."

They rearranged quickly, Coop stacking a couple of pillows behind his head as he settled on his back and rolled the condom down his length. He smiled at Beau as he carefully swung a leg over his hips. He took a moment to just admire Coop, his strong chest, wide shoulders, and firm abdomen. He didn't have a six-pack, but he was solidly built, no doubt from some form of manual labor.

He almost asked right then what Coop did for a living but bit back the question, leaning forward instead and kissing across his chest. The last thing he wanted was to make Coop uncomfortable by trying to get him to share information he didn't want to give him.

Staring into Coop's dark blue eyes as he started to sink down on his cock, he felt a sudden ache in his chest. No matter how amazing Coop made him feel, this weekend was all Beau would ever get.

Swallowing down the heavy emotions building in his throat, he promised himself he'd take anything Coop would give and savor it. He refused to regret anything that happened between them.

The burn as he took Coop inside him was intense, but in a way that made him feel like he could feel every cell in his body at once. And he never wanted it to stop.

Once Coop was buried all the way in him, Beau took a shuddery breath, eyes closed.

Strong hands gripped his hips. "Okay?"

"Mmhmm." He nodded and gave his hips a swivel, grinning at Coop's soft curse and opening his eyes. "Just enjoying how good it feels."

Coop kept his hands on him, but he didn't guide Beau's movements or try to control how fast he went as he started raising and lowering his body. He began slow and sensual, loving how big and thick Coop felt inside him, but he couldn't keep the pace for long as his desire ratcheted higher.

He was really riding Coop, staring down into his eyes with his hands planted on his firm chest, when Coop grunted out, "Yeah, sweetheart, use my cock to forget him."

Beau nearly fell off his dick he was so surprised. Was that what Coop thought he was doing? "He's already forgotten," Beau whispered. "There's no one here but us."

Something changed in Coop's face, a softness appearing around his eyes and mouth as tension eased from his jaw. He drew Beau down for a sweet kiss, then smirked at him. "Good. But I still want you to use my dick to feel good."

Sucking in a breath, he shivered and nodded. "Yeah, okay. I can do that."

Coop couldn't seem to stop himself from running his hands over Beau's body as he started moving again, like whatever had been holding him back was gone, and now all he wanted was to experience every moment as fully as possible.

When Coop thrust up suddenly, Beau cried out and fell forward, his whole body lighting up with entire constellations. "That felt…"

"Yeah," Coop agreed, wrapping his arms around Beau and rolling so he was back on top of him.

Beau moaned at how the movement jostled Coop's erection inside him and then again when Coop rearranged them. They ended up with Coop on his knees, his hands gripping Beau's calves tightly so his heels were pointed toward the ceiling.

Then he thrust for real and Beau couldn't breathe.

As amazing as it had felt to sink up and down on Coop, enjoying the fullness and setting whatever pace he wanted, scratching at the sheets beneath him as Coop plunged into him hard and fast was a hundred times better. It was like Coop's cock was made for Beau, his big, round head hitting Beau's prostate over and over.

There was so much precum leaking from Beau's untouched erection it looked like he'd already come. As the pleasure rose higher, his body tightening deliciously, he grabbed at the pillow under his head and arched his neck.

"Oh god, just a little faster. I'm so close," he moaned.

Instead of speeding up, Coop came to a stop and moved both of Beau's legs to one side, resting his calves on Coop's wide shoulder and wrapping an arm around them. Achingly slow, he withdrew, then thrust back in hard.

Coop hissed and did it again. "Fuck. Your ass is so tight this way. I feel like I can barely move inside you."

All Beau could do was moan and feel every inch of Coop sinking inside him. Coop sped up once more, sweat dripping from his furrowed brow as he used his free hand to grab Beau's cock and give it a squeeze just under the head.

It was like being struck by lightning, heat and electricity and fire racing through his body. His ears were ringing, and he couldn't stop crying out in agonized pleasure each time Coop's hips hit his ass.

His orgasm built so suddenly and exploded so ferociously out of him that he screamed, head thrown back and eyes squeezed shut.

He could hear Coop grunting with each thrust as he chased his own release, but it was like he was floating on a cloud, the bursts of pleasure radiating from his ass and groin keeping him flying high.

All the air was squished out of him when Coop collapsed on top of him, but he didn't really mind. He forced his heavy arms up and around Coop's back as they both tried to catch their breath.

"Whoa," he finally murmured.

Coop grunted in reply, but he also pressed a kiss to Beau's throat, so he didn't take offense.

He didn't even have time to worry about being ruined for sex with anyone else before he passed out.

CHAPTER TEN

By unspoken agreement, they pretty much stayed in bed all of Sunday, the soft ticking of the clock on the wall like a thundering countdown when they lay next to each other and silently stroked exposed skin. Coop could only handle the sound for so long before he was rolling on top of Beau once more and kissing and touching him until he was breathless. It was like he suddenly couldn't get enough now that he'd decided to let himself enjoy however much time they had together.

Coop knew from experience that a plow truck would reach him either later that night or early the next morning, having finally finished the more populous areas. Though he'd never had quite so much fun being snowed in before.

Trucker interrupted them every few hours, bored and wanting attention, but Beau would just laugh and cuddle the big baby when he crawled between them in bed. In the afternoon, they both took him out, Beau bundling up in some of Coop's extra outerwear and spare pair of boots. Everything was enormous on him, and it made Coop's chest ache as he watched Beau try and throw the large sticks Trucker brought them, struggling under the weight of Coop's heavy coat and laughing when he nearly fell.

What if we could really have this?

The thought had speared into his brain like an arrow, souring the happy moment. He knew better than to even suggest keeping in touch after Beau left. The story Beau had told him the day before about his college boyfriend had taught Coop two things: first, Beau had terrible taste in men. Like, so bad.

But the second thing was that if Beau wasn't even willing to consider moving for a man he'd dated for nearly two years, he'd never be on board with long-distance dating Coop. Especially because Coop would have to make it clear from the beginning that he couldn't do it for long. There would be no way he'd handle only getting to see Beau every once in a while and then trying to be happy with texts and phone calls the rest of the time.

Not to mention, despite what Beau had said the night before about Danny the Douche being forgotten, Coop knew that couldn't possibly be the case. No matter how crappy their relationship had been, Beau was still mourning the loss of the future he'd been planning with the guy. Coop understood what that was like, to have all your carefully orchestrated plans torn to pieces and left to be blown away by a strong wind.

Beau would need time to heal from the pain of Danny's betrayal and figure out what he wanted moving forward. Coop couldn't be an anchor holding him down, nor would he settle for being a reminder of the worst moment of Beau's life.

If something were to happen between them, he wanted Beau to *choose* him, not just find what they had as convenient or cling to Coop so he wouldn't be alone again.

Even if Beau did choose him... what was the point? Coop

couldn't just pack up and move his business, and Beau wouldn't move away from his dad.

There just wasn't a way for them to move forward.

He forced himself to push the idea out of his head as best he could and savored every moment they did have together. Was it fair that after years of convincing himself he was done with dating, he had the perfect guy fall into his lap… only for him to live on the other side of the state?

No, but who said life was fair?

Coop watched Beau long after he fell asleep completely sated and with a small smile on his face, and finally let his mind contemplate the idea of what a life with Beau could look like. He imagined there would be a lot of sex, but there would also be a lot of quiet moments and laughter and Beau falling on his ass because he was a bit of a klutz.

And lacy panties.

And long walks with Trucker.

And cooking all of Beau's favorite foods and watching him enjoy every single bite like they were the best things he'd ever tasted.

Coop had spent the last ten years building his furniture-making business up to a pretty damn successful endeavor. He loved working with his hands and creating things that people loved and cherished, knowing they'd be passed down through generations. He'd originally opened the place with his uncle, the person who'd first taught him how to appreciate a good piece of wood and turn it into something amazing.

Things had been a little bumpy at first, but eventually they'd built up their clientele and improved their marketing. It had gotten to the point where he'd needed to hire more help a few years back because his uncle's arthritis had started to slow him down. His best friend, JP, had convinced him to bring on his youngest brother, Junior, as an apprentice.

He'd been worried about ruining his friendship if it didn't work out with Junior, but he hadn't needed to because Junior was a beast. No problem working hard and took directions like a champ.

The two of them had been working so well together that his uncle had actually retired last year out of the blue. One day, his uncle had been watching Coop and Junior work on a piece together, and then he'd laughed, clapped him on the shoulder, and told them Coop he didn't need him anymore.

But what would happen if Coop eventually moved closer to Beau? Would Junior come with him? Would his clients be willing to travel hours to pick up pieces?

Or would he lose everything by chasing after a man?

A voice in the back of his head—and he was sure this time it was his sister—told him that he was being fatalistic, needed to calm the eff down, and consider that maybe things would work out if they were meant to be.

Meant to be. What was this, a *Hallmark* Christmas movie?

He eventually fell asleep too, thoughts still twisting and turning in his brain, giving him weird dreams about chasing a plow truck being driven by a faceless man that he somehow still knew was Danny the Douche.

A rumbling sound woke him around five, his eyes burning and brain foggy with exhaustion. It only took a moment for the sound to make sense though, and dread filled him.

A plow truck.

The countdown was over. Time was up.

He was sprawled on his back, but lifting his head, he found Beau curled up on his side next to him, facing away. Breath catching in his throat, he turned and fit himself to Beau's smooth back, burying his face in his neck and chuckling roughly when Beau woke squirming.

"That damn beard feels amazing in other places, but it's

just ticklish there," Beau murmured, nestling farther into the bed.

"Other places like between your ass cheeks?" Coop asked, voice husky from sleep and arousal. His dick was making a valiant effort to rise to the occasion, despite how many times he'd come the day before and well into the night.

"Yes, you perv," Beau muttered, wiggling his butt against Coop's groin but then settling back down, his breaths evening out once more.

Smiling, Coop pressed a kiss to the love bite he'd left on Beau's neck late yesterday and rolled away. Beau made a soft sound but didn't wake back up.

Trucker was already standing next to the bed on Coop's side, head resting on the mattress and eyes hopeful. Even though it was over an hour before they normally got up, his silly dog was totally up for going out in the cold.

Two hours later, Coop stomped his boots off on his porch and glanced over his shoulder. He had a plow for the front of his truck and a snowblower that he kept in the tiny garage next to his cabin. He'd been able to clear out the driveway, even stealing Beau's keys again and moving his car out of the way so the whole thing could get scraped clean.

Now Beau's shiny Lexus was sitting just at the bottom of the stairs, facing the road. Ready to take Beau away from Coop and his simple cabin in the woods.

Shaking off his morose thoughts, he finished cleaning the snow off himself, then stepped inside, surprised when he didn't see Beau in the kitchen or living area. He stripped off his outerwear, petted Trucker where he was curled up on the couch, and headed back into the bedroom.

It didn't look like Beau had moved a muscle despite the racket Coop had been making outside.

Unable to resist the temptation of Beau's naked body even though it was covered by the sheet and blankets, he stripped and crawled back into bed, crowding against Beau's back once more.

Shuddering, Beau tried to squirm away. "Oh my god, why are you so cold?"

Coop didn't bother answering, just tried to sneak his chilly hands down to wedge them between Beau's thighs. Beau squealed and flailed, trying to get away. Their laughter —and Trucker's barks from the end of the bed, when he came flying in to see what the ruckus was about—filled the whole room, the whole cabin, with a lightness and happiness Coop hadn't experienced in… a long time.

When they finally settled back down, him on his back and Beau plastered to his front, head on his chest, Coop stared up at the ceiling as his mind warred with itself. He wanted to throw caution to the wind and beg Beau to give him a chance. He knew it was dumb for a number of reasons—not least of which was Beau's engagement being so newly broken off. What if Beau had just wanted a fling to get back at Danny, and now he was going to go back, throw the sex in his face, and then work things out?

He knew that was bullshit—at least the part about Beau using him and getting back together with Danny. If anything, Beau would use the boost he'd gotten in self-esteem to find someone a hundred times better than Danny the Douche. Someone who would love his sexy ass, sweet smile, and tendency to chatter.

Someone who would get Beau a dog of his own to love on whenever he wanted.

"Coop?"

He hummed, tightening his arm around Beau's shoulders and taking a deep breath to try and settle his racing thoughts.

"Do you think… I know you said…"

Coop narrowed his eyes when Beau trailed off and

pushed his face into Coop's chest hair like he could possibly hide from him. "What is it, sweetheart?"

His heart wanted Beau to be brave enough for both of them, but his mind was skeptical his luck was that good.

Beau raised his head after a few moments and peered down at him in the early morning light. Finally, he said softly, "Never mind," and lay back down, fingers gripping at Coop's skin almost too tightly.

He didn't push. As much as he wanted to, wanted to beg and plead that Beau stay the rest of the week so they could figure out how to make something work between them, he knew that wasn't fair. Beau needed time to get over Danny, and Coop would never be another asshole who mistreated him.

They stayed in bed for another hour, bodies pressed together and breathing nearly synchronized, before Beau sighed softy and sat up. He gave Coop a sad smile before climbing out of bed and heading for the bathroom.

Coop was almost mad when he watched Beau's ass jiggle and his dick didn't even stir. He was trying so hard not to push Beau for something he wasn't ready for and was devastated at the idea of him leaving. It was all too much emotion for his dick, apparently.

Stupid thing. Hadn't it gotten the memo that the weekend was supposed to be just about good sex? No feelings were supposed to be involved.

Grumbling, he stood and pulled on his sweats again, leaving a fresh pair and a T-shirt for Beau on the end of the bed. By the time Beau stepped out of the bedroom, Coop had a stack of pancakes and sausage links ready. He tried to smile at Beau when they sat at the table and started eating, but it felt more like a grimace, so he was betting he'd failed. Only the corner of Beau's mouth twitched in return though, so he knew he wasn't the only one not able to put on a brave face.

"I take it the roads are clear?" Beau finally said as they were finishing up, his gaze locked on the window behind Coop's head. The one that faced the driveway. The now plowed-out driveway.

"Yeah. Came through about five this morning." Coop stood and started to clear the table, emotions stuck in his throat and making it impossible for him to eat the last few bites on his plate.

Before he was ready, the kitchen was cleaned, and Beau's suitcase was repacked and zipped tight, sitting next to the door. They were both staring at it, seemingly frozen. Trucker sat at Beau's feet, whining softly, and it broke Coop's heart into even more pieces.

Crouching down, Beau wrapped his arms around him. "It's okay, sweetie. You and your daddy can go on even more walks now that he doesn't have to take care of me. Maybe even use that ice fishing shack I saw sitting on the lake yesterday."

At the side-eye he got, Coop chuckled hoarsely. "Yes, sir. More walks, and I'll take him fishing."

Beau kissed Trucker's head and stood, swiping beneath his eyes. "And play fetch with him even if he brings back sticks that are too big."

Coop just nodded, unable to speak at the sight of Beau's wet lashes.

"And slip him some treats under the table sometimes. He's a good boy and deserves—"

He couldn't take it anymore. With one step, he was pressed to Beau's body and stealing the words from his mouth with his tongue, taking his lips in a hard kiss. The broken sound Beau made as he clutched at Coop's shoulders echoed in his ears.

By the time he ripped his mouth away to catch his breath,

he was convinced he'd been about to make the biggest mistake of his life. Thankfully, it wasn't too late.

"I know you need time after your breakup to figure things out," he started, speaking slowly and choosing his words carefully, "but I want a chance, Beau."

"A chance?"

"Yes. A chance to be with you. I'm going to give you my number." Beau's brows furrowed and he opened his mouth, but Coop cupped his face and kept going. "If in a month you feel the same way—that what we shared here was special and deserves to be explored—I want you to let me know, okay? I know it would be complicated, but I… I want a chance."

Beau stared at him with bright eyes. "I thought you didn't do relationships anymore," he whispered, fingers clutching at Coop.

"So did I." He shrugged and leaned down, pressing their foreheads together. "But this adorable guy with a thing for my dog showed up at my cabin in the middle of a blizzard and convinced me otherwise."

"He sounds smart." They both laughed softly, the air between them filling with excitement and possibilities. "I'm glad you didn't leave me out in the cold that night."

"Me too." He gave Beau one last, lingering kiss. "I hope I hear from you in a month."

CHAPTER ELEVEN

"You know this is insane, right?" his dad said, standing behind him and blocking the doorway of his bedroom.

Beau finished zipping his suitcases—he'd made sure he had actual pants this time and smiled at the memory of wearing Coop's all weekend—and straightened, turning to give his dad a reassuring smile. Tall, handsome, and always dressed well, his dad cut an intimidating figure, but not to Beau. To Beau, he'd always be the guy who ran out onto the field when Beau was in little league and he'd been crying on the field after tripping over second base and spraining his ankle. His dad had raced out to him, calmed him down, and convinced him not to quit on the spot.

"I know you think so, yes. You've made your opinion very clear." Beau walked over and gave his dad a quick hug, then nudged him out of the way and slipped past him.

"You barely know this guy," his dad said, trailing after him and spouting the same things he'd been saying all week, ever since Beau had told him he was moving to Knotting Pines to be with the man he loved.

After leaving the cabin, he'd made it three days before he'd sent Coop a text, asking if he really had to wait a month to talk to him. Coop had called him that evening, and they'd talked on the phone for three hours. Coop had told him about his family, and Beau had shared about his mom. Then the next night, he'd called Coop, and they'd spoken for two more hours, Coop telling him about his uncle and his business. At the end of the first week, he'd asked Coop if he could come and visit him, but Coop had been reluctant, convinced Beau was still getting over Danny and wasn't ready for a new relationship. Beau hadn't agreed, but he hadn't pushed, realizing that maybe Coop was the one who needed more time to get used to the idea of them being together.

So they talked every night, and Beau learned all about Cooper Frances and his life in Knotting Pines. After the third time of Coop complaining about bookkeeping, Beau also knew what he'd be doing for work if he could convince Coop to let him stay.

Four weeks after driving away from the cabin with tears running down his face, he knew Coop better than he knew anyone in the whole world, and he was beyond ready to see him in person again. To hold on to him as Coop kissed the daylights out of him. To walk in the park with him and Trucker. To feel Coop inside him again.

He was almost positive Coop wouldn't turn him away when he showed up.

Almost.

Butterflies erupting in his belly, he took a deep breath as he double-checked that he had everything he needed. He'd left most of the living room and kitchen stuff for the movers he'd call Monday if things went well. God, he hoped they went well.

"Beaumont Singer."

Uh-oh. His dad *never* used his full name because he knew

how much Beau didn't like it. He turned slowly, eyebrows raised. "Yes?"

"You can't just go gallivanting after some guy because the sex was good," his dad said, using his serious voice and crossing his arms over his chest.

Beau made a face. "Gross. Don't talk about my sex life." And it was *phenomenal*, not good, but he wasn't going to share that. "This is happening. I'm twenty-five—you don't get to make decisions for me anymore, Dad."

Face getting redder and running a hand through his perfectly cut hair, his dad pegged him with a fiery look. "What if he says no? What if he hurts you like Danny did and I'm not there again?"

"Dad." He rushed over and hugged him, suddenly feeling like crap for being so excited to see Coop again that he'd forgotten he would be leaving his dad behind. Face smashed against his dad's chest, he said, "You trust me, right?"

His dad sighed and tightened his hold on Beau. "You, yes. This... *Coop* guy? No."

Snickering, he leaned back and looked up. "You have to trust that I know what I'm doing."

When all his dad did was give him an unimpressed look, Beau laughed and patted his arm as he stepped away.

"You can come and visit whenever you want as long as you promise to be nice," he said, double-checking he'd cleared out his fridge. It was Saturday morning, and he wanted to load up his car so he could head out, but his dad was really slowing him down.

His dad grumbled something behind him, but Beau ignored him, grabbing a couple of bags and heading for the door. There was a lot of huffing from his dad, but he managed to hold his tongue as they carried his suitcases and bags down to his car and packed everything in the trunk and back seat.

When he was ready to head out, he turned to his dad and gave him another quick hug. "It's going to be weird to be so far away from you," he whispered, then pulled back and wiped at his eyes.

"You can come home whenever you want," his dad said, his voice rough with emotion.

"I know."

"And you'll be seeing me soon," his dad added just as Beau was about to climb into his car.

He paused and gave his dad a questioning look. "Oh yeah?"

Pretending to examine his nails, his dad said, "One of the project managers pitched a housing development idea that would be right outside that tiny town *Coop* is from."

"You said you were passing on that project." Beau remembered because he'd recognized the area in the proposal, having already familiarized himself with Knotting Pines and the surrounding towns. But he definitely hadn't brought it to his dad's attention that it would be so close to where he was moving because he knew his dad would do exactly what he was doing. Use the project as an excuse to keep an eye on Beau and Coop.

"Changed my mind." His dad gave him a blinding smile as he stepped away from Beau's car. "See you in a couple weeks."

"A couple weeks!" But his dad was already turning away, whistling softly as he hurried in the cold February air to his Mercedes-Benz CLS parked in Beau's guest spot. "That devious bastard," he muttered, sliding behind the wheel of his car and pulling the door closed. He was sure his dad had waited until Beau had told him he could come visit to deliver his news.

As his dad pulled away—throwing one last cheery wave at him—Beau refocused on what he was doing. He was about to drive two hours to tell a man he hadn't seen in person in a month that he was in love with him and wanted to move in with him.

No biggie.

His heart started to race as he navigated traffic, but by the time he got on the highway, he was calming down. As scary as the prospect of rejection was, he knew he had to risk it. None of the men he'd dated before had ever made him feel as safe or cared for as Coop had in the first twenty-four hours he'd known him. Coop was special, and the way he made Beau feel was special.

He couldn't lose that because he was scared.

He'd hyped himself up by the time his GPS told him he was at his destination, so he didn't hesitate to climb out of his car and stretch his back out. The house he'd arrived at was outside of Knotting Pines on a little bit of land. Two stories with a bare porch on the front, it looked nice, but the large barn just past it was what drew and held Beau's attention.

He knew from his many conversations with Coop that was the place he'd find him at eleven o'clock on a Saturday morning. The big red barn was where he housed his business, and he had an office where he worked on invoices and paying bills every Saturday so he didn't get behind.

All Beau had to do was walk inside.

Yup… that was it.

For some reason, his feet weren't moving. He was excited to see Coop, and all he wanted to do was run inside and jump into his arms, but the tiny kernel of fear that he was making a mistake kept him frozen in place. Not even the wickedly cold wind whipping past him was enough to move him.

"Worst day ever?"

Beau whirled around, breath catching in his throat at the

sight of Coop in the same red plaid coat and black knit hat he'd had on the first time Beau saw him. His hair was a little longer, peeking out under the hat, but otherwise he looked the same as Beau remembered: perfect.

He was just in front of his truck… which was parked behind Beau's car. How the heck had he missed Coop driving up behind him?

The words Coop had greeted him with circled in his head, but it took a long moment for him to realize that it had been the first thing Beau had ever said to Coop at the cabin.

Smiling, he shook his head and took a step forward, absently noting the bag of fast food in Coop's hand. "Nope. Best day ever."

Coop raised a brow and slowly took a step too. "Why's that?"

This was it. This was the moment he'd been dreaming of for weeks. He couldn't mess it up, or he'd regret it for the rest of his life.

"Because today I get to tell the man I love how I feel about him and ask him to let me live here with him."

Coop froze a foot away, eyes widening in surprise. "Live here?"

Trying not to be deterred by Coop not responding to his declaration, he straightened his shoulders and nodded, pointing at the suitcases in his car. "I remembered pants this time."

Following his arm, Coop eyed the full back seat, his mouth twitching. "That's quite a few pairs of pants."

"I'm hoping to stay quite a while."

"Hmm." Coop took another half step forward. "With the man you love."

"Yes," he rasped out, unable to look away from Coop's steady gaze.

"Does he love you back?"

Sucking in a breath, he slowly nodded. "Yes."

Coop's mouth finally tipped up in a smile. "Good answer, sweetheart."

Then Coop was throwing his bag of food onto the trunk of Beau's car and wrapping his strong arms around Beau. His cold lips claimed Beau before he had a chance to do more than clutch at the front of his coat.

God, he'd missed this. He couldn't hold back his whimper as Coop cupped the back of his head and deepened the kiss, swiping his tongue inside.

"I've missed you so much," Coop murmured against his lips, nipping his bottom one playfully. "I nearly got in my truck twenty times in the last month, intent on tracking you down and holding you in my arms again."

"Every time we hung up, I almost called back to beg you to let me come see you."

Coop huffed as he slid one hand down to slip under Beau's coat and find the edge of his jeans, dipping a finger inside. "I'd have caved. God, you don't know how many times I jerked off staring at your lacy panties, thinking of you wearing them."

"You kept the ripped ones?" Beau asked, shuddering at the picture Coop was painting in his head.

"Oh yeah," Coop murmured, scraping his beard down Beau's neck and pulling the collar of his coat aside to bite playfully at his throat. "I can't believe you're finally here. And you brought your things so you can stay."

"All my clothes and electronics. The rest of it the movers can bring… if you're okay with me moving in."

Nodding, Coop raised his head. "It's kind of fast. Are you sure?"

"More than sure. Nothing and no one makes me feel the way you do, Coop. I love you so much."

Coop's grip became almost painful with how hard he

squeezed Beau for a moment. "Fuck, I love you too. So damn much."

"Good answer," Beau quipped, grinning wider than he ever had before, not evening caring that he'd forgotten his hat in the car and his ears felt like they were turning into ice cubes.

Chuckling, Coop released his hold and turned to grab his abandoned food bag. He wrapped an arm around Beau's shoulders and started toward the house. "Come one, sweetheart. Let's get you out of the cold."

"Okay," he whispered, letting Coop lead him up the porch steps, Trucker's excited barking coming from the other side of the door.

There were still plenty of things he wasn't sure about regarding his new life and relationship, but one thing was plenty clear.

It really was the best day of his life.

Thank you so much for reading Out In The Cold! If you enjoyed Beau and Coop's story, please consider leaving a short review on Goodreads or Amazon.

You can find another sexy story about blue-collar guys from Knotting Pines in Laying Pipe*! Plumber John falls for his best friend's son, Lukas, and has fun exploring his new-found bisexuality.*

NEXT BLUE COLLAR HEARTS

LAYING PIPE

John

John has a good life. A mostly happy one even. It's simple and a little lonely at times now that he's divorced, but that's okay. Not everyone is destined for a great love or happily ever after.

But he does have a thriving business and a best friend who's like family. What more does he need?

Definitely not his best friend's son. Even if John *did* look at men that way, there was no way he'd risk his friendship because he'd suddenly noticed things about Lukas he never had before.

Like how sweet he was. Or how good-looking.

Or how much he wants to kiss him…

Lukas

Having a crush on his dad's best friend for years hasn't done wonders for Lukas's love life. No one ever quite measured up to the kindhearted man who always seems to be there when Lukas needs him.

He knows nothing can ever come of it since John's

straight. Like, used to be married to a woman, only ever dated women, super blue collar kind of straight.

Not to mention, his dad would lose his mind…

But it's totally fine! Lukas is sure he'll get over his feelings eventually.

Even if John is suddenly *looking* at him differently.

Almost like… Almost like he wants to kiss Lukas?

That can't be right.

Laying Pipe is the first in bestselling author Kiki Clark's Blue Collar Hearts series. It features a 42-year-old plumber who's good with his hands... and pipes, a 26-year-old vet tech with the softest of hearts, a late-blooming bisexual, super low angst, and butt-touching as a love language.

Available on eBook, Paperback, Audiobook, & KU!

EXPAND YOUR TBR!

RECKLESS is the first in my Leather & Chrome series which focuses on the Devil's Hands Motorcycle Club and the exploration of kinks. Tank and CJ's story features a prison pen pal program, an age gap, exhibitionism, and a tough biker only soft for his kinky virgin.

Available in eBook, Paperback, Audiobook, & Kindle Unlimited.

THE ALPHA AND HIS KING is the first in my paranormal romance series—The Kincaid Pack. Each book features fated mates, a dash of angst, big found family feels, and slow burns that burn hot, hot, hot!

Available in eBook, Paperback, Audiobook, & Kindle Unlimited.

FREE KINCAID PACK PREQUEL

A NEW PACK FOR NEW YEAR

Free to download at www.kikiclark.com/newsletter

Injured and terrified, Victor runs for his life and right into the arms of the last person he expected to find: his true mate.

Living in a pack who viewed imperfections as weaknesses that needed to be eliminated, Victor is lucky to escape alive. He's heard of the Kincaid Pack's strong but fair alpha, but he has trouble truly believing he won't be targeted once more if his shameful secret is discovered.

When Cole meets a young man with fear in his eyes and pain in his scent, he recognizes him as his mate on sight. His excitement is short-lived, however, when they find out Victor's life is still in danger from what his old pack did to him.

After a lifetime of being abandoned by others, Victor has an important decision to make: Will he choose to trust the mate fate gave him?

Or will he run again?

A New Pack for New Year *is a prequel to the best-selling Kincaid Pack series and features an eighteen-year-old wolf in need of some TLC, a thirty-something lion dying to give it to him, sexy times in an inappropriate place, found family feels, and hurt/comfort that will warm all the corners of your heart.*

ALSO BY KIKI CLARK

Blue Collar Hearts Series

Out In the Cold (Beau & Coop)

Laying Pipe (John & Lukas)

Kincaid Pack Series

FREE Prequel: A New Pack for New Year

The Alpha and His King (Rick & Kai)

The Second and His Bonded (Kieran & Bennett)

The Deputy and His Enforcer (Marcus & Robson)

The Hunter and His Mates (Drake & Jamie & Gabriel)

The Enforcer and His Heart (Nico & Keegan)

Kincaid Pack Adult Coloring Book Vol 1

Leather & Chrome Series

Reckless (Tank & CJ)

Temptation (Six & Ollie)

Yearning (Houston & Kenneth)

Leather & Chrome Holiday Story

Joyful (Rooster & Emmett)

Forever Family Trilogy

Favor (Declan & Jeremy)

Scythe Series (co-written with EM Lindsey)

Until His Last Goodbye (Elias & Tristian)

Prequel Novellas

Until His Beginning Ends

Until His Soul Awakens

Available on Audio

The Alpha and His King

The Second and His Bonded

The Deputy and His Enforcer

Laying Pipe

Reckless

Temptation

ABOUT THE AUTHOR

A small town Michigan girl, Kiki has enjoyed reading since she first picked up Harry Potter and the Sorcerer's Stone as a child. After that, she devoured everything she could get her hands on and dreamed of one time writing her own books that touched people's hearts.

In her early twenties, she discovered LGBTQ romances and had a realization: these were her people and this was where she belonged.

Nearly ten years later, she's proud to finally join the ranks of authors releasing character-driven, emotionally satisfying books showcasing that everyone deserves to find love.

To keep up-to-date with Kiki, sign up for her newsletter: http://www.kikiclark.com/newsletter or join her Facebook group: https://www.facebook.com/groups/kikiskorner.

Keep in touch by following her on any of these platforms:

facebook.com/kikiclarkauthor
twitter.com/kikiclark_
instagram.com/kikiclark2017
amazon.com/author/kikiclark
bookbub.com/authors/kiki-clark
goodreads.com/kikiclark

www.ingramcontent.com/pod-product-compliance
Lightning Source LLC
LaVergne TN
LVHW020648100826
845148LV00012B/2382